P9-CAN-726

1. URSULA K. LE GUIN, The Visionary *and*
   SCOTT R. SANDERS, Wonders Hidden

2. ANAÏS NIN, The White Blackbird *and*
   KANOKO OKAMOTO, The Tale of an Old Geisha

3. JAMES D. HOUSTON, One Can Think About Life
   After the Fish is in the Canoe *and*
   JEANNE WAKATSUKI HOUSTON, Beyond Manzanar

4. HERBERT GOLD, Stories of Misbegotten Love *and*
   DON ASHER, Angel on My Shoulder

5. RAYMOND CARVER and TESS GALLAGHER,
   Dostoevsky (The Screenplay) *and*
   URSULA K. LE GUIN, King Dog (a Screenplay)

6. EDWARD HOAGLAND, City Tales *and*
   GRETEL EHRLICH, Wyoming Stories

7. EDWARD ABBEY, Confessions of a Barbarian *and*
   JACK CURTIS, Red Knife Valley

EDWARD ABBEY

Confessions of a Barbarian

VOLUME VII

CAPRA PRESS
1986

Cover design by Francine Rudesill
Designed and typeset in Garamond by Jim Cook
SANTA BARBARA, CALIFORNIA

LIBRARY OF CONGRESS CATALOGING-IN-PUBLICATION DATA
Abbey, Edward, 1927-
CONFESSIONS OF HENRY LIGHTCAP, BARBARIAN.
(Capra back-to-back series)
No collective t.p. Titles transcribed from individual title pages.
I. Curtis, Jack, 1922-   .   Red Knife Valley. 1986
II. Title.   III. Title: Red Knife Valley.
PS3551.B2C6   1986   813'.54   85-26939
ISBN 0-88496-244-X (pbk.)

PUBLISHED BY
CAPRA PRESS
Post Office Box 2068
Santa Barbara, Ca. 93120

CONFESSIONS OF A BARBARIAN

EDITOR'S PREFACE

While on a brief lecture tour through the American Southwest—barbarous territory—I encountered the narrator of the book which you hold in your hands.

Escaping early from a tedious reception at the home of a departmental chairperson, one of those standardized affairs in which the limp monologues of assistant professors of regional literature peter out beneath the bibulous libidos of faculty wives, I settled at a corner table—alone at last—in the "lounge" of my Holiday Inn. I loosened my tie and prepared to enjoy the hour supreme—myself.

Where was I, otherwise? It hardly mattered: Austin, Texas? Albuquerque, New Mexico? Tucson, Arizona? Boulder, Colorado? Salt Lake City, Utah? I find these provincial towns indistinguishable and derive comfort from that fact for reasons similar, not to say analogous, to the pleasure I find in the universal homogeneity, dull, plain, adequate and thoroughly dependable, of Holiday Inns, Mr. Marriott's hotels, Mr. Hertz's motorcars.

Waiting for a waiter or waitress (or waitperson) to arrive, I looked once again, with satisfaction, at my lecture notes: "Parallels and Pitfalls in the Proto-Fiction of Willa Cather and the Meta-Fiction of Susan Sontag." The lecture had been well received, as indeed it has been received well everywhere west of the Hudson River, if one may interpret total silence as close attention, and a certified check for $2,500, autographed by the secretary of the Board of Regents, as a sign of approval. I so choose to construe it. What Willa Cather herself—now happily retired to Heaven, where she had always wanted to be—might think of my analysis of her work one can merely conjecture; but I have been the recipient of indirect signals from close associates of my other author suggesting that Ms. Sontag, quite omnipresent among the living and still hoping to grow up to be a Frenchman, is not entirely displeased.

The bar was crowded, the service negligent. I looked about for a cocktail waitress, spotted one but failed to catch her attention. I found instead that I was the unwelcome object of interest in the leering eyes of an extremely attenuated, hollow-cheeked country-man—a "redneck," as they say—perched on the synthetic fabric of a revolving chair at the bar itself. I met his dark, smirking, knowing look for only a moment—caught by my own catlike curiosity—and quickly returned my attention to my notes. One thing I've learned in my years on the college speaking circuit: never make eye contact with a bore. And I can recognize a bore not merely instantly but instantaneously—particularly the type I've come to identify as the *scintillating bore*. But it was too late.

Pretending a scrutiny of my notes, I became aware of a pair of long legs clad in dirty denim and copper rivets standing close by my left elbow. I felt the little eyes squinting down at me, the unpleasant grin on the loose lips. Another peasant aesthete; I know the breed. Although "breed" is hardly the proper term; "sport" or "mutant" would be more correct, as befits the product of generations of ignorance, isolation and incestuous intercourse.

I feigned unawareness of the creature's presence. Useless evasion.

"You're Abbey," he said.

I looked up, reluctantly. He leaned high over me, a potential tower of babble at least six feet four inches in narrow-framed, extennuated height. Not simply the type but the stereotype, the archetype (ah! but I know it well!), of the Appalachian mountaineer—inbred, ill-bred, genetically degenerate. The goofy grin on his mouth, the crackpot gleam in his eye, did nothing to allay my initial bad impression or soften the snappiness of my judgment.

"Edward Abbey," he said. "Famous unknown author, etc."

"That's only hearsay."

"Don't kid me. I've read your crap. I know your line. We're onto you, Abbey."

"If you don't mind, sir..." I shuffled my papers. "I am rather busy at the moment."

"This is a bar, not your office." He sat down on the opposite side of the booth and fixed me with his lunatic stare. "Never drink alone," he said.

"One sometimes prefers that."

"Oh, one does, does one?" His mocking grin was hostile; I feared physical danger in his bad manners, the tics and tensions under his skin. "Listen," he went on, "I ain't got much time here. Let's talk business."

"I'm not aware that you and I have any business to discuss."

"Oh Jesus listen to that. I've read your books, Abbey. Why be a failure all your life?"

"What? What's that?"

"I mean I got something here—" But he halted.

The cocktail waitress had finally discovered us, friendless, forgotten, alone at an arid table. She was of the kind the unlettered call "pert" and/or "sexy," wearing—*que typique*—a costume of vulgar brevity. Victim of habit, I said to my uninvited guest, "You like bourbon, no doubt?" He nodded. To the young lady I said, "Two J.W. Dants, please, on the rocks, with water." She started to leave; he touched her arm.

"Bring me the same," he said.

She nodded and pranced away, rosy cheeks aglow.

He watched her retreat, smiling in unabashed admiration. "My God, Abbey, wouldn't you love to slip the old bone into that?"

I ignored what was no doubt meant as a rhetorical inquiry; the subject, in any case, is one the importance of which has been unduly exaggerated in the contemporary hedonic empire. Taking advantage of the man's slack-fibered distraction, I studied his appearance with greater care. The study of appearances is, after all, a basic function of my appointed task in life. Appearances tell us little or nothing of underlying reality, to be sure; but the overlay is the surface on which, perforce, we skate through life, is it not?

I estimated his age at forty-eight to fifty years. His hair was thick, coarse, blue-black as an Indian's but with streaks of gray at the "temples"—i.e., those flat surfaces beneath the forehead and before the ears. His eyes were small, deeply sunken in their gaunt sockets (premonitory of the fate which, in our bodily capacity, awaits us all), the irises gray-green and strangely, feverishly, unwholesomely bright. His snout or nose, most striking feature in an otherwise undistinguished face, was large, with the high thin bridge of a bird of prey—aquiline, an eagle's beak, its fleshy parts revealing the fine red lines of alcoholic indulgence. The man's cheeks, as mentioned before, were sunken, concave beneath stark cheekbones, and the jaw haggard, quite lacking in the comfortable jowls appropriate to a man of middle middleage. He had dark, Appalachian skin more sallow than brown, in texture leathery, suggesting excessive exposure to the ill effects of wind and sun. He needed a shave; an unseemly furze of frosty gray and dingy black whisker added nothing of aesthetic value to a face in need of whatever cosmetic aid modern science and medical technology can provide. In bodily frame, to conclude, he appeared stringy, gaunt, much underweight for a man of his unusual vertical extension. A small pot of a belly overhanging his belt did nothing to dispel the overall effect of dysfunctional leanness in the relatively narrow shoulders, shrunken hams, rack-stretched thighs. The man was not long for this world. But then who is?

He turned again to me. "Abbey," he said, "what I want to tell you—"

"Sir, I don't even know your name." Or want to know it, I thought. But an instinctive caution led me to delay for as long as possible the broaching of the matter which I guessed—had guessed already—was parboiling on his cramped but excited brain.

He offered his right hand. I took it. It felt like the forepaw of a crocodile—bony, scaly, all claw. Grimy fingernails. "The name is Lightcap," he said, "Henry Lightcap. Lightcap by name and Lightcap by nature. But what I want to tell you is I got something here that'll make you rich and famous. And me too."

Oh dear. I knew of course what was coming. I'd seen the bulky package under his arm when he sat down at the table. I recognized from oft-repeated experience the familiar shape of yet another 1,000-page unpublished and unpublishable manuscript, another maudlin, mendacious and meandering autobiographical novel. The curse of Saul Bellow, Thomas Wolfe, Charles Dickens, Tobias Smollett—and Job. (Author of the world's first picaresque novel). Everywhere I go, the impertinent importunity. I can't relax in any public bar without some naive layman coming to me, sooner or later, with this proposition: So you're the writer, he says; well listen to my tale, it'll knock your spats off, I tell it, you type it up, we split the proceeds fifty-fifty, neither of us will ever have to work for a living again, etc.

I looked up at the crazy greedy eyes of this intruder—even sitting down he seemed to loom over me, and I am a man of more than average height myself, with good posture and confident mien—and I said, "My dear sir: I am an author and a critic (the two not always mutually exclusive), but I am not a publisher."

"I'm an author too," he said, as expected. My heart sank, but before I could respond the cocktail waitress returned, tart, saucy, two-thirds naked, a thoroughly obnoxious specimen of her sex, and deposited four oversize highballs on our table. Lightcap's eyes, as if attached by invisible wires to the young woman's plump backside, once again attended her departure. "God," he muttered, "I'll bet she could chew peanuts with that."

There was no apparent limit to the man's capacity for vulgarity. Not only his rough hands, not only the soiled gray flannel underwear revealed by the open collar and rolled-up sleeves of his shirt, but even his words, his tonal inflections, carried about them the odor of the barnyard—or as they say in these parts, *partner,* the "rank and acrid stench of the corral."

Again he turned to me, the loose grin exposing strong but plaque-covered, yellowish, crooked teeth, behind the teeth a deeply-fissured brain tongue of a lavender hue. (Further token of hereditary degeneracy.) "Ed," he began—

"My friends," I interjected, "call me Ed. I prefer to be addressed formally by others."

That checked him only for a moment. Grinning the patient, cajoling grin, as if he were dealing with a retarded child, he began again. "Abbey," he said, "I'm not asking you—"

"As a matter of fact, sir, I've been awarded the academic degrees of both Ph.D. and Litt. D. You may address me as *Doctor* Abbey."

It distresses me to be compelled to resort, on occasion, to such directness. But insolence must be crushed, wherever it appears.

"Okay, Doc," he said, "and I got a master's degree in screw-worm metaphysics. You can call me Master." Setting aside the first of his two tumblers, which he had emptied in brief spasmodic swallows, Adams apple throbbing in long red neck, he laid his package in its padded book-mailer on the table between us. I looked at the obscene thing with dismay. Another square, thick book. It would have to be at least a thousand pages long, probably single-spaced, perhaps even scribbled out in longhand. "You'll like this," he said, his mouth rehearsing again its exaggerated, exasperating rictus of fake good will and fraudulent good fellowship. "All you have to do is read ten pages, that's all I ask, and you'll be hooked, gripped, *snatched,* like an old whore backing into a doorknob. Ten pages, Abbey—Doctor Abbey, pardon me!—that'll turn the trick. You can publish the thing under your own name, Christ, I don't care, you need it more than I do." He paused; gave me his *earnest* look. "You've been in a rut for a long time, Abbey, trying to write like those East Coast androgynes—Gardner, Cheever, Irving, McPhee, Updike, all those johns. It's time you left them behind. Them suburban chic-boutique arthers."

I looked into his manic-expressive eyes, fascinated in spite of myself by the reckless foolishness of his manner. Of course he was conning me. Still, I lacked the courage to tell him that I too now resided in the Far East. Not entirely in disagreement with his implied judgments, I said, "When the sun of literature is low even the smallest figure casts a long shadow."

"That's a good line. But Schopenhauer said it first."

"Of—course."

He finished his second drink and shoved his package toward me. "Read it, Abbey."

I stared at the thing, quite unwilling to commit myself to any such disagreeable task. I prepared my usual evasive words of demurral. "My dear Mr. Lightcap...really...."

He stood up abruptly, kicking back his chair. I braced myself for an act of violence. The false smile gone, he looked down at me from his grotesque height with the bleak, dismal, contemplative detachment of a vulture. "Then don't read it," he said. "Burn it. Throw it to the dogs. Wipe your ass with it and eat it. Make 1,200 sailplanes and flip them off your penthouse roof, what the hell do I care. Don't bother me no more."

He turned and strode to the outside door, pausing only once, at the service bar, to drop a few words into the attentive ear of our cocktail waitress; she smiled, looked up at him and nodded. (Bitch. Slut. Tramp. Whore.) Then he was gone, out into the cold, windy dreadful night of this dreadful Western city, whatever it was. I heard the rumble of an engine, the roar of a ruptured muffler....

I remained for some time at the table, sipping gingerly at my drink. I don't care for bourbon whisky, actually—gin is the writer's preferred refreshment, or was until recent years, when other and more genteel beverages became the vogue—but had ordered the foul stuff on a momentary whim, betraying the silly urge to ingratiate myself—why?—with that raffish eccentric whose odor yet haunted the other side of the booth.

The book, the man's wretched book, mute and totally un-appealing, lay in its grease-stained brown wrapper on the table, awaiting the decision which I knew I had already made. I paid the bar tab, leaving a minimal tip, tucked my lecture notes in my inside suitcoat pocket, and retired to my room, carrying the bulky package under my arm. Let the chambermaid see to the final disposal of this *opus vulgus*; the man Lightcap would no doubt have an extra copy stored away. Meanwhile I might, for lack of anything better to do in the bland void of my "Holy Day" Inn, take a casual glance at a few pages. . . .

Not many; I had a plane to catch at 8:25 next morning.

*   *   *

Very well then, it has been agreed and decreed that these *Confessions of Henry Lightcap, Barbarian,* be published. With some misgiving and considerable reluctance, I have allowed my name to appear on the title pages as "editor" of this memoir, if we may so call it. My title is not unearned; the reader will be pleased to learn that the book has been trimmed, reduced, rendered down, to less than half its original length. This was not difficult, since so much of the original typescript consisted of the author's compulsive accounts of his numerous—perhaps innumerable—sexual adventures, each and every one a trite, banal, repetitious, drearily conventional exercise. It was with pleasure, I assure the reader, that I excised this marbling of lubricious lard, allowing to remain only those scenes and liaisons which seemed necessary to the structure of the narrative and the portrayal of the novel's central figure.

Lightcap calls this shambling monster an "honest novel." A novel in the form of a memoir, or memoir in the form of a novel, "honesty," whatever that means, is hardly the criterion. The term "novel" (more old than new) does not properly apply here either. If a novel, it is the baggiest sort; if a story, shaggy as an Airedale dog. Call it a book, since it now appears between covers— inadequate cover. If meant as a work of fiction, it violates every rule of substance and organization which critics have succeeded in abstracting from the compost of literature. A novel, we now know, is essentially a *symbolic structure,* complete in itself, self-referential in every aspect, a coherent system of semantic signs corresponding not to objects or events in the so-called "real world" but to the inherent integrating principles of the work itself, as I have shown in my discussions elsewhere on the *crisis-cruxus-nexus* syntax of ante-post-modernist anti-fiction. In short, symbol and symbol symbolized become, through the alchemy of art, identical, i.e., as in the congruent identity of content and form. The subject of literary art therefore is seen to be no other than art itself; the technique of art and the art of technique—they are one!

One what? you ask. You may well ask. But shouldn't. For the answer is implicated in the question itself.

Such considerations diverge to a depressing extent, I fear, from the world of Henry Lightcap. After skimming his badly typed and barely legible script, I shipped it by Federal Express to my publisher, urging him not to publish so retrograde a work. I regret to say that I was over-ruled, and consented to play the editor's part in this production only when so induced by an advance against royalties of such extravagance that I could neither, in good conscience, refuse my editorial services, nor, out of modesty, disclose the exact monetary figure at this time on these pages.

Has Lightcap's book any literary merit whatsoever? No; none whatsoever. Why then publish such rubbish? The chief reason has been alluded to above: commercial greed. But one further and less than merely incidental apology may be suggested: this "novel" has a certain antiquarian value, or if not value then interest, in that in its pages we can contemplate, in the person of this Henry H. Lightcap, an American type now totally anachronistic. I do not mean extinct. They persist, alas, these atavists, throwbacks and living relics, in various dark grimy pockets around the nation, wallowing like pigs in the *boué* of their animal-like refuges, gathering from time to time—amidst the whining schmaltz of "country music"—in their "family bars" and "honky-tonk" saloons and "cantina contentas," then appearing regularly at state Department of Employment Security agencies to apply for unemployment compensation checks. But they are outmoded, they are obsolete, they are culturally, economically, politically and sociologically retrogressive.

There is no place for such awkward, abrasive and non-productive anarchs as Lightcap and his brother Will in a well-ordered society of high technology, high culture, haute cuisine, high-density population, and high, not to say higher, sexual, metaphysical and religious aspirations. Some may find this techno-evolutionary culling-out a matter for regret. I do not. Nostalgia for the frontier mode of life is understandable but no longer intellectually respectable. Such attitudes impede the full flowering of our civilization. The Henry Lightcaps of America, like the redskinned buffalo-hunting horsemen of the West, had their day—a century ago! They are the final incarnations of the Vanishing Americans. Let us let them vanish.

It is the one sole merit of Lightcap's *Confessions* that it enables us to grasp, between thumb and forefinger as it were, how little our loss entails.

Enough, you cry, about this unfortunate book and its unhappy author's kind. What of the man himself? How has he reacted to the publication of his work? What is he doing with that fresh filthy money, etc.? Yes, I understand the drift of the reader's true interests and am glad to satisfy them. The answer is that Henry Lightcap the man appears to have disappeared. That is, we have so far been unable to locate him in the space-time continuum. Three years have passed since that encounter in the bar; not a word have I received from Lightcap himself.

Goodness knows, in preparing the contract, the publisher and I made vigorous efforts to find our author. There was, as it happens, no address or telephone number given on the manuscript of the book or on the mailer in which it was enclosed. Attempts to reach Mr. Lightcap through a certain cocktail waitress at a certain Holiday Inn were fruitless; she too was gone, leaving no forwarding address. Investigating the alleged locale of much of the story, I could find neither the village of Stump Creek nor a Shawnee County in the state of West Virginia. Granted, the entire Appalachian region, from northern Georgia up through western Pennsylvania, is inhabited by numerous descendants of the family Lightcap, but none has come forward to present himself as the author of a book—any book. Inquiries made to the "University" of New Mexico, where Lightcap received his higher education (he is, as he confesses, an auto-didact), and to the National Park Service and the U.S. Forest Service, of which governmental agencies our man was once a frequent if only seasonal employee, have brought us computerized responses verifying Lightcap's existence as a pre-recorded entity on floppy disk, microfilm and silicon chip, but no knowledge of his present whereabouts.

However, despite his odd abstention from current events, Henry Lightcap's interests have been provided for: his ten percent (10%) of the advance on royalties has been placed in an escrow fund, available on demand by the author at any time within one year after the ratification of my contract with the publisher (which said event was duly consummated in a simple, informal ceremony in the Oak Room of the Plaza only ten months ago) after which time, as we decided is customary in such cases, all royalties and other author's proceeds from publication of CONFESSIONS OF HENRY LIGHTCAP, BARBARIAN, hereinafter referred to as THE WORK, will be paid to the editor of aforesaid WORK, namely and to wit the undersigned, i.e.,

—Edward Abbey
Sagaponack, NY

IN MEDIAS RES, ARIZONA
April 1980

I

● ● ● **S**lamming the door behind her. Slams it so hard the replastered wall around the doorframe shivers into a network of fine reticulations, revealing the sleazy hand of a non-union craftsman.

I listen to her booted feet stomping over the graveled driveway, into the carport. (The "car-port"!) Then the vicious brittle *clunk!* of car door likewise slammed. God but that woman has a temper. Shocking. Now the thunderous roar of four-cylinder Nipponese motor starting up, the squeal of spinning wheels, the yelp of a startled dog as she skids around the broomplant, past the dead saguaro and down the lane toward the street. Past the mailbox and fading away, out of my life again forever, into the dim intense inane of Tucson, Arizona.

I can see police helicopters circling—blinking red like diabolical fireflies—above our doomed, damned, beleaguered city. Red alert. Elaine is on the loose.

19

Woman. Wo-man. Womb-man. Woe-man.

Easy come easy go. My first and no doubt false reaction is one of relief. An immense and overwhelming sensation of blessedness. There never was a good war or a bad peace, as Abe Lincoln said. (We had similar troubles.) I sink slowly into my easy chair, hers actually, but it's all mine now. Probably.

Gloating, I look around "our" livingroom. Our "living" room. All those books jammed in their shelves—all that B. Traven and R. Burton and M. Montaigne and James M. Cain & Co., all them Sibelius Stravinsky Shostakovitch Schubert records etc., Waylon & Willie & Whatshisname (Hank Williams), that stereo, that 1922 Starcke upright grand pianoforte and I do mean forte, the Franklin stove and the "Persian" rug (mfg'd in Pakistan) the leatherbound basket chairs from Mexico, that big solid blond slab table of California sugarpine, a masterpiece of the joiner's art, nothing but dowel pegs and butterfly joints, not a nail or screw or touch of glue in the whole thing—wealth. I am rich, rich, beyond all my dreams of avarice, at least for the next few days or until her attorneys get to work on me. Who will it be this time? Pleasant & Frost again? Or Connive, Finagle & Krones, who knows?

And so forth. When I hear the word "settlement" I reach for my checkbook.

The power of property. I will sell everything in this house in the next twenty-four hours, everything that's not bolted down, convert our goods into something better, cash, and buy a cheap houseboat on Lake of the Ozarks. No, Lake Tahoe. I have always wanted to live on a houseboat. No rent, no mortgage payments, no gas, sewage, garbage, phone or electric bills, live on catfish and bluegill, grow a hydroponic garden of my favorite vegetables—the carrot, the potato, the bean, the turnip. Can't think of any others. But they exist.

Henry indulges himself in a favored phantasy. I shall live the clean hard cold rigors of an ascetic philosopher. A dive into the icy lake at dawn. Two quick laps around the shore. A frugal breakfast of cool water and unsalted watercress, followed by an hour of meditation. And then—then what? What then? Then I'll row my houseboat ashore, jump into my rebuilt restored 1956 Lincoln Continental 4-door convertible and speed away to the nearest legal whorehouse for some quick fun & frolick before lunch.

The GM Frigidaire in the kitchen, that giant and neurotic machine, starts revving its engine. Sounds like a Boeing 747 warming up for takeoff. I've never known a refrigerator that works so hard at keeping cool. The jarring noise disturbs, as it always does, my fake and uneasy calm. For two years I've been living in the same house with this monster and I'm still not accustomed to it. I never will be.

The noise increases. An ugly hatred grasps possession of my soul. I march to the bedroom, take the revolver from under my pillow, enter the kitchen, confront the machine. Vibrating, roaring, the Frigidaire presents to me its bland broad bronze-colored front. On the door panel a bunch of magnetic letters have been arranged to spell the words "Fuck you Henry." I raise the revolver—a .357 magnum—cock the hammer, fire. Point blank, right through its smug face. A black round hole appears in the center of the door, the letters slide down a few inches but maintain rough syntactical order:

Fu ck y o uH e r n y

My ears ring from the sound of the blast. And what's more the engine continues to bellow. Well, of course, the engine's at the bottom of the thing, generating heat that seeps upward into the interior. And the walls, in order to provide greater inside capacity, are no more than an inch thick. No wonder it has to work so hard. Any properly designed refrigerator would have the motor on top and exposed, dissipating its heat toward the ceiling, and the walls would be at least three inches thick, like a safe. Like my Aunt Ida's antique Kelvinator back in Morgantown, West Virginia.

Losing its cool through its new nostril, the Frigidaire roars louder than before. Or am I hallucinating? Going down on one knee, taking no chances, I fire into the base—once, twice— through the grill into the motor into the bowels the guts the living drooling quivering glands of the machine. The cogs whimper to a halt, shutting down the condenser and compressor; strands of black smoke and the smell of Freon issue from beneath. I think I've hit some vital parts. But now I hear the buzzing of a stalled electric motor. Sure, I could simply pull the plug, cut off the Frigidaire's life support system. Would be the merciful thing to do. But I want to *destroy* this mad molecular motherfucker, fix it so it never breathes again, never again grates on the tranquility of a contemplative mind. I poke the muzzle of my piece through the shattered grill, into the furry dust and black widow cobwebs of its underparts, and point toward the buzzing sound. Pull trigger—

BLAM!—and there's the screech of lead slug, hollow-pointed and dilate, smashing through a clutch of copper coils.

Silence.

That does it. I've settled this bastard's hash. Relieved, I rise to my feet and tuck the revolver into my belt. Peace. Stillness. A beauteous calm reigns in my kitchen, except for the usual background noise, from the city, of a diesel freight train clattering down the rails, of the endless caravan of forty-ton Peterbilts, Kenworths, Macks, Whites, Fruehaufs grinding along the Interstate, of Air Force jets screeching through the air a hundred feet above the campus of the University of Arizona, reminding those pointy-headed professors and idle scheming students who—or rather, What—is really Boss around here. But that, as I say, is only ambience, like the shrilling of the evening crickets in the weeds, the ringing in my ears. I close the kitchen windows, the better to enjoy my freedom. The refrigerator takes off again.

The noise this time comes from the top of the machine, from the fan and defrosting mechanism, thermostatically activated, in the rear of the freezer compartment. A separate motor? Evidently. There are two rounds left in my handy handgun; I open the freezer door, shove aside the frozen chicken and frozen boxes of Lean Cuisine (Elaine's dietary regime) and blast two holes through the fan vent behind the ice trays in the back wall. The little fan scratches to a final stop. I dig a handful of ice cubes from the ice cube tray and fix myself a drink. My hands are shaking. But not from this trivial bit of shooting.

How can she do this to me? Damn her anyway, how can she be so cruel, so heartless, so—violent? At such a time, with total disaster weighing on my heart? You picked a fine time to leave me, Elaine. How could she know about that? You had a month to tell her and you never quite got around to it. But ignorance is no excuse. Godamn her, how could she be so cold and bitter and full of hate?

Familiar emotions. I've been through this ordeal before, a number of times. I know the schedule. First the abrupt departure and my immediate sense of liberation and relief. That passes quickly. Next comes the anger, the rage, of which our defenseless Frigidaire has been the first victim. (I look around for other targets. That electric range with its console like the dashboard of an airplane? Adds twenty dollars to the light bill every month. The automatic pop-up toaster which always burns my toast? The Sony Tee Vee in the bedroom—that national lobotomy machine? The washer-dryer set in the bathroom? A dryer! an electric dryer! in the hot arid clime of southern Arizona. That electric water heater in the closet with no exterior on-off or temperature controls whatsoever? "DANGER: Do Not Remove Access Panels or Attempt To Reset Thermostats Without Assistance of Licensed Electrician." What else? The air-conditioning unit on the roof? Another expensive, repeatedly malfunctioning, bloodsucking incubus on my life. How about the telephone on the wall, unplugged at the moment but always a threat?)

Relief followed by outrage. Those are the first two stages. The third stage is the worst and it will come soon enough, probably about three o'clock in the morning: The Fear. The Terror. The Panic—awakening in the dark to find myself, as I had dreamed and dreaded, alone.

That will come. Meanwhile we've got a half quart of the Wild Turkey to see us safely past midnight. And if that fails? I draw the revolver from my belt and look it in the eye. I tilt the muzzle toward my face and try to see down into the black infinity of the rifled bore. The thought of suicide, as Nietzsche says, has got me through many a bad night. Like this:

$$\left[\ \left\{ (\ \odot \ ) \ \right\} \ \right]$$

Absolution.

I put my ultimate tranquilizer away. Some other time, perhaps. In fact, knowing what I know, knowing what I have been told and shown, there's no perhaps about it. The natural right of self-slaughter. Always a viable option, a good working alternative. Sometimes the only sensible solution. No other animal on earth enjoys so free a choice. The ascent of Man. No one has a right to complain about life because no one is compelled to endure it. Who said that?

I look around the silent kitchen. There's nobody here but me and in the freezer, beginning to thaw, the frozen chicken. Life is hard? Compared to what?

Yes, I'm aware of the objections. But those who formulated the ukase against voluntary oblivion are the same who gave us the Inquisition, the iron maiden, the rack, the wheel, the iron stake and the auto-da-fé. The same who gave us (and how can we ever thank them?) the doctrine of Hell, of everlasting torture by fire under the benevolent eye of an all-seeing all-knowing God of Love. While the saved look down with satisfaction at the agonies of the damned.* Nothing in human history, not the Gulag, not Beuchenwald-Auschwitz, not Hiroshima-Nagasaki, can compare in total horror to the eschatology of the medieval Christian theologian.

But as to that, who cares anymore?

Brain-sweat. My brain sweats like this all the time, secreting thought. Maybe you wouldn't call it thought, hardly worthy of that designation, but—ideas. Ideas about ideas. I talk to myself continually, even in my dreams. A genius is always on duty. Like the drip-pan under the Frigidaire, always needed. How overcome anxiety? Try fear.

You accuse me of self pity. What of it? A little self-pity never hurt anybody. It's a protective mechanism. Pretty soon now the Agent Orange, the Zyklon-B will be rising through the tendrils of my nervous system, up from the bowels like swamp gas, like sewer gas, and into the antechambers of the heart. I remember the sensations well from the last time—was it only three years ago?—when Whatshername? Myrna? Mara? Moira? Myra?—walked out on me, also slamming the door. A different door but identical symbolism. Not that I remember every detail of the pain, any more than a mother remembers completely the discomforts of childbirth—there's no substitute for the real thing—but well enough, as one recalls the associated misery, the concomitant anguish. Not the pain itself—but the pain of the pain.

---

*"It is not sufficient that we be blessed," say the elect; "it is necessary that others suffer horribly."

She's not coming back this time. Godamn her, how can she do this? Do this to me, who never meant her any harm, who blundered along as best he could, always with the best of intentions. Ahead lies another long dark night of the soul. Her parting gift: despair. And so on, that much is clear.

But enough, enough, let's hear no more whining and mewling. Buck up, man, you've got troubles more interesting than another divorce to think about. E.g., your job, in peril once again. Your little secret. Your immortal soul.

Time for palliatives, ameliorants, placebos. I rise from my chair, somewhat numb and wooden, and choose a record album from the shelf. Wolfgang Mozart, Gustaf Mahler or Willie Nelson? Ernie Tubbs or Palestrina—old pal of mine. I feel the need for something hearty. Soul music. I stack the spindle with the Resurrection Symphony, flip switch, turn volume up to nose-bleed capacity and retire hurriedly to the shelter of the kitchen. The first great magnificent chords blast through the walls and rumble up my back-bone at the rate of $33\frac{1}{3}$ revelations per minute. Good man, Gustaf . . .

Yanking down the bourbon bottle, I pull the cap and take a quick preliminary suck, like calf at cow, before refilling my glass. Easy on the ice. A dash of the branch from the tap, good old Tucson City Water, rich in trichloroethylene and other well-known industrial solvents. My hand is shaking. Remember your glands. Easy, easy, got to taper off on this stuff, all things in moderation, there's less than half a bottle left. Courage: God will provide. Paracelsus called it the elixir of life. Delusions, certainly. So I'll get shitfaced fallingdown snotflying toilet-hugging drunk. We'll manage anyway won't we?

Tough questions which I am not prepared, at this point in time, to answer.

Mahler. Bourbon whisky. What else is available? Music begins where words leave off but even music is sometimes not enough. Trapped in my own soap opera, I yearn toward grandeur—but not grand opera. Not those screaming sopranos, those tensile tenors, that athletic caterwauling, that gymnastic howling of the damned: grand opera is a form of musical entertainment for people who hate music. No, what I want is a quiet, decorous, classical tragedy with a few belly laughs thrown in for fun. A farce with funeral.

What else is on hand? The telephone. The telephone hangs there on the wall in mute black Bakelite. Lifeline. Hope. Reach out and grab somebody with a drowning embrace, a strangle-hold of want. Godamn their eyes. I plug-in the thing and open my book of numbers. It's Will I'd like to call, but pride forbids. He ain't heavy but he's my brother. Maybe later. What you really need, when the horse throws you—

The phone rings. At once, out of habit, I unplug it. When I want electronic communication I'll initiate it myself. I'm in no mood for taking calls from unidentified parties. The ideal telephone is the one-way telephone. Don't call me I'll call you. Maybe. Evil things. That one we had before, you couldn't unplug it. Wired into the wall connection. And if you left the receiver off the hook for more than 30 seconds it began squealing at you like a pika in the rocks. A devilish instrument. I used to wrap it in towels and stuff it in a drawer. But still I could hear it ring. I tried packing it inside the freezer of the refrigerator but the cord, small as it was, let cold air leak out. I put the thing in the sink under six inches of water. That silenced it, alright, but also ruined it. That's when I demanded and got a plug-in phone from the godamned phone company. A twenty-five dollar installation charge came with it; outraged, I demanded a fifty percent cut in the monthly rate since the phone would be used for outgoing calls only. Mountain Bell refused to negotiate. I refused to pay. My wife snuck out behind my back and paid the fee herself.

I find the number I'm looking for and replug-in the bloody phone. It's ringing. Still ringing. God Almighty—maybe it's Elaine, smitten by remorse. Or Kathy or Susan or Heather or Valerie or Whatshername, having heard already, somehow, that I'm single again. "All pleasure consists in variety," said Sam Johnson. Maybe it's my mother. Or brother Will. That's how they get you by the tender parts. The ghost of hope. The possibility of family trouble. Alright, I take it this time:

"Lightcap here."

"Good God Henry I've been trying to get you for ten minutes. Your phone's always busy. Are you okay?"

"Who's this?"

"It's me—Joe." My next door neighbor, McReynolds. "I thought I heard gunfire."

"I heard it too, Joe, off in the brush out back. Some gun nut."

"Did you call the police?"

"What good would that do? I went out and ran him off myself. Sicked the dog on him. Excuse me, Joe, I've got to hang up on you now." I close the connection for a moment, lift the receiver and quickly dial my number. Her phone rings. Rings again. Phone ringing in an empty room. Bell ringing in an empty sky. Kathleen, you tricky little fox, where are you when I want you? No answer.

Hang up, unplug phone. Think. I could call this lawyer I know.

His estranged wife is picking his bones, he's as angry and helpless as I am. Morris, I could say, I'll murder your wife if you'll murder mine. We'd both have perfect alibis. Be a hundred miles away in a public gathering when the crime takes place. And not even a crime in this case, except in the narrow, legalistic sense of the word, but a public service. Our good deed for the day. Deeds, not words. At least if Elaine were defunct, suddenly murdered or run over by a cement mixer or struck dead with an aneurysm, I'd not have to suffer so much from guilt. My sense of loss would be modified, mollified, pacified, with little injury to pride.

Contemptible sentiments. I'm ashamed of myself.

Open bottle, pour. Whom should I call?

Mahler plunges into his second movement, the angels appear above a thunderous barrage from the kettledrums; the march macabre in bass viols of the *Dies Irae* booms through the house. We'll have no resurrection yet, not until sides three and four. Another fifteen minutes of burial alive.

If only good sweet Sandy was here. A reliable rainy-day woman. She could cure my blues anytime, pull me up from the black plague of the blue malaise, whether the straight funk, the deep funk, the deep purple funk, or the melan-colic. She'd pull off my shirt and jam my head in the kitchen sink, shampoo the scruff from my scalp and soul and dry me off with her long hair, drag me down to the rattan mat on the floor and knead my neck, back, shoulders, pull my pants off and massage my buttocks, thighs, calves, feet, then lash my bare body up and down, back and forth, with her mane of wet, heavy, maple-golden hair until the static electricity crackled with every stroke. When my hard-on became so enormous it was jacking me up from the floor I'd roll over, clutch her in my tentacles, force entry into the handiest orifice, and fuck her with every digit until our ears began to bleed. God, Henry, she'd moan, you're like an octopus, you're into everything at once. If I'm an octopus, I'd say, you're my octopussy.

Santa Fe. Land of Moab. The West Desert. Death Valley. that was ten, fifteen, or was it twenty years ago? She had a little two-year old boy named Scott, spoiled rotten. An obnoxious midget. Jealous, he hated my entrails. His favorite trick, when Sandy and I were totally inter-involved, was to come crawling over us with his diapers dripping baby shit, bawling like a banshee. Scott the Snot. I was tempted many a time to flush him down the toilet bowl, put him out of his neurotic miseries forever. Sandy betrayed me anyhow, finally, by slipping around to see her husband. The last time I saw her she looked so beautiful I hardly recognized her. Should not have said so aloud.

I had to let her go. But we're still friends. Unfortunately she lives 600 miles away. San Diego, for godsake! That submerging suburb of Tijuana. . . .

Handy home remedy, that's what I need. Should I call one of my nearby friends? Check off the list? No, not tonight, not yet. Show a little pride. Don't run panic-stricken into the streets. You'd hate yourself in the morning. Well, if not one of them, how about a crony? Shelton? Arriaga? Ferrigan? Lacey? Let them be, it's late, near midnight already, and Mahler's only halfway through, you've got to hear him out, common courtesy. Music, music, song without words, the ultimate sea. I'd give ten years out of my adolescence to be able to play the banjo, the fiddle, the slide trombone—to beat the tympani for Zubin Mehta and the New York Philharmonic.

I notice now that the oven light is on. That woman, she's left the oven turned on again, no wonder it's so bloody warm in this bloody stinking kitchen. But the little red bulb gives me an idea. Inspiration strikes. I'll bake a loaf of bread. My wife has fled, our dog is dying, my job hangs by a thread, God and Nature have betrayed me, there's no Sandy here to shampoo my hair, no Kathy to floss my teeth, no Honeydew Mellon to tease my wits, I'll fool them all and bake another loaf of bread. That always helps, not much but some, and right now I need all the help I can get. (*Ayudame! Succor! A'l'aide! a'l'aide!* out of the heat and into the shade.)

Mahler roars in the living room like a caged lion, romping through his grotesque scherzo, and then comes that *little phrase,* that repeated cheerful happy little phrase, like a man whistling in the dark, that lifts and always lifts my heart—for a minute or two—into the empyrean realm of Rocky Mountain air, as near to Heaven as I'll ever get, up there high among the aspens, the immaculate white trunks, their green-gold trembling leaves, their feminine rustling in the morning wind. . . .

Nervous—or nerveless-numb anyway, hands quaking like the mountain poplar, I get out bowls, wooden spoons, measuring cups, yeast, milk, butter, salt, sugar, flour. Real flour: Hungarian stone-ground whole wheat. Best commercial flour available. Old Will, naturally, that proud pompous sonofabitch, grinds his flour in his own little hand mill, mounted to a 500-pound butcher's block. Sometime tonight I'll write the letter:

Will. Dear Will. Listen, farmer, I'm in trouble again.
Need some help. Would you mind if I dropped in for a
month or two or three or four? . . .

I mix the yeast in water, stir, set aside for a moment. Mix warm milk and melted butter, add the foamy yeast, add salt, sugar, stir again. Sift and sprinkle in the good nut-brown flour, the crunchy wheat berries, and mix with wooden spoon in the big wooden bowl. Thinking of the green green grass of home. Of Will—he ain't heavy he's my brother. Of our tough sweet beautiful mother, quietly but indomitably vigorous at 78, walking the hills, doing her work, leading that cracked geriatric choir at church every Sunday morning. She apologized for the imperfections. You sound like angels, I assured her. Yes, she said, we are getting close to Heaven, aren't we? Thinking of home. Yes, I know, home is where when you have to go there you probably shouldn't. So what. The animal knows best.

Knead your dough, compadre. Sprinkle flour on the rolling board, fold the fat warm living dough into its own center and mash it down with heels of both hands, firmly but gently—don't bruise the living yeast cells—over and over, working the outside through the inside, topside out the bottomside, a topological wonder of Moebiusian marvels, over and under and round and round until everything is satiny smooth as a baby's bottom.

I grease another bowl with butter, flop my great glob of pale-brown breathing dough into it, cover with damp dishtowel and set on top of Fridge, over the hot-air vent, under the ceiling. Now let it rise, double in volume, a genuine resurrection, an authentic miracle. Which was the worthier technological achievement, the moon-landing or the invention of bread? The bake oven or the nuclear reactor? Can there be any question? Only a fool would hesitate to answer.

My Frigidaire is strangely quiet and generating no hot air. Stone dead—for a moment I'd forgotten. I contemplate its fatal wounds with pleasure. This chingadero is definitely defunct. Nothing more satisfying than a gut-shot refrigerator. Down with General Motors. If Will can do it I can do it. Cut the lines. Break loose. Blast free. Someday. . . .

I fantasize a speech: Men: how long shall we tolerate this two-headed mechanical kraken (U.S. & S.U.) draped upon our world, its rubber tipped tentacles probing every asshole, proctoscoping every colon, palpitating every prostate? Kitchen full of clamoring appliances, heat pump-air conditioner bellowing on the roof, the Tee Vee with its perpetual soul poison in full living color, the home computer locked in to Central Control, your heads wired to microwave relay (as R. Buckminster Fuller had often urged), this creeping cobweb of wires lines cables pipes conduits semi-conductors that keep us bound, like the Laccoön, in the strangling coils the boa constrictors of technotronic tryanny, etc. Blow it away, I say. Now or never. Bust out into the open, into the wind.

(No response. Are they dead out there? And does it matter? In a nation of sheep one man makes a quorum.)

Mahler winds down, fading into reverie. Time to invert those disks. Refilling my drink—long night ahead—I advance to the stereo, turn the records and retreat quickly to the kitchen before the twin speakers catch me in their convergent blast. But this is the fourth movement (out of five), not a great baying of horns but a gentle female wave of choral voices *pianissimo* . . . . Ethereal but real, celestial but terrestrial as well.

Weeping in my whisky, I return to the kitchen. In music lies the ideal world, the closest we'll ever deserve to get to immortality. Whether it's Mahler or Louis Armstrong, Gregorian chants or Japanese bamboo flutes or some grog-rotten Celt on yonder bonnie ridge braying like a jackass through his bagpipes loud enough to raise the dead—it's resurrection. Temporary but true, like life itself. Inspired, I plug in the phone and dial Doctor Harrington, M.D. My friend, always on call.

"Andrew?"

"Big Hank? It's late, Henry. For you. Why aren't you in bed with your loved ones?"

"Andy, I need a recipe. An antidote for pain."

"Try agony."

"I tried that. This is worse. Can't sleep, Andy."

"Well, read a book. Read some—Balzac. Or George Eliot or Anthony Trollope or Thomas Hardy. One of those awful Victorian novels."

"I tried that. It's dull."

"All great art is dull. How about George Gissing?"

"I'm baking bread."

"Ah hah! So she's left you again."

"Again? For good this time. Andy, I hear the wings of death flapping over the roof. Foul green shit is trickling from the air ducts."

"I see. Keep talking."

"She's moved in with Whatshisname. That computer science professor."

"Sounds indicative." A pause. "Well, Henry, you had fair notice."

"A computer science professor!"

"Yes. I know. They're everywhere, aren't they?" Another pause. "But she tried to tell you. Anyone could see it. What did you expect?" No answer. "Come on over, Henry, I'll sit up with you. I can't sleep either, as a matter of fact."

"Can't, Andy, my dough is rising." I looked; indeed it was. Doubled in size.

"Well," he says, "don't do anything weird. Get rid of those damn guns. Call one of your old girl-friends. Bake your bread, take some aspirins, and go to bed. That'll be thirty-five dollars please."

"Listen, Harrington, I don't need good advice, I need some pills. Real potent pills. I feel lower than whale shit."

"What're you drinking?"

"The same old stuff."

"No pills tonight. Dangerous. Turn your tube on, they're showing *Treasure of Sierra Madre* on Channel 9, best movie ever made. Turn your tube on, keep drinking, take three aspirins, fall on the floor and get some sleep. Have lunch with me tomorrow."

"Sure, Andy."

"Call me in the morning. Or I'll call you. Don't disconnect on me." Pause. "You hear me?" Pause. "Henry? You still there?"

"Still here."

"Maybe I should come over there. I could sleep on your couch. You want me to come over there? I'll bring another bottle and we'll celebrate together. What do you say?"

"No, I'll see you tomorrow. Got to knead my dough now. Thank you anyhow very much. Goodnight, Andy."

"Be careful."

I hang up. At once the phone begins to ring. I unplug it and take down the bread, the warm sweet dough and lay it on the board. I love this part too, folding and refolding the pneumatic voluptuous pregnant living dough. I punch the air out, rolling it over and over, shaping it into a nice fat oblate blob, and place it in my greased baking pan. There. Now. Back to the refrigerator top, warmest spot in the kitchen. Let her breathe and swell for another thirty minutes. The staff of life. Thy rod and thy staff. Comfort. Flagons, apples, bread. And thou beside me in the sunshine on the warm pine needles eight thousand feet above sea level on Cape Royal, Point Imperial, the Kaiparowits Plateau. (Myra! Honeydew! Claire!) *Elaine?*

Maudlin malarky. The whisky and ice percolating through my kidneys, time to relieve some pressure. I stumble to the bathroom, flicking switches as I go. Conserve power. Keep the utilities in trouble. Hastily unzipping, I whip out the old uncircumcized roto rooter and piss into the washbasin. Perfectly sanitary, urine is sterile, much tidier than pissing into the toilet bowl from the male position, splashing hot piss over the rim and floor and rug and shower curtains. Could've pissed in kitchen sink, yes, but the sink is full of dirty dishes again. What a slob that woman is. Was. Well now, with her gone, we'll have some *ordnung* around here, some "ordered liberty," as our neo-Fascists like to say. What's worse than a knee-jerk liberal? A knee-pad conservative, that's what, forever groveling before the rich and powerful. Anyhow, we'll have stability now, control, discipline, centralized administration, that's the thing.

The face in the mirror grins at me. Little squinty eyes with veins of gaudy red, like Christmas tree baubles. Jaw bristling with whisker—needs a shave. Hair greasy as a groundhog. Man needs a shampoo. Whole ensemble looks neglected. Need a shit, shave, shower, shampoo—probably a shoeshine. Nevertheless, I think, no matter what, by God, I still don't look as bad as I feel. Nor feel as bad as I look.

I shake and squeeze it, trying to expel that final golden drop. Fail, as always. The last jewel trickles down my thigh when I pack the thing back in its nest. Sign of middle age, perhaps. The old pipe organ—tireless tool—betrays the first faint symptom of incipient senility. The dotage of the dong. The Grim Raper falters. What of it. For thirty-five years, ever since boyhood, I've been bound in servitude to this *thang* (sic) with a mind of its own—but no conscience—leading me about by the nose. Like a dog straining on a leash. Nothing but trouble. I'm tired of it. Thirty-five years of sexist hoggishness, now I want some tranquility. Simplicity. Serenity. The comfortable stupidity of the contented, that's what I crave. Down with romance.

Check the bread. Almost ready for the oven. A few more minutes. Now what? Shall I call Ingrid in Denver? Lynell in Santa Barbara? Candace in Cambridge? Becky in Seattle? Nancy in Phoenix? One o'clock by the clock—better not. The bitching hour. They wouldn't understand. What would brother Will do? What would Tolstoy do? Mann? Russell? Diogenes? Henry David Thoreau? Mark Twain? Francois Villon? Rabelais? Montaigne? J. Prometheus Birdsong, all my heroes dead and gone?

Alas there is no remedy. No shampoo by Sandy, no vicious delicious tongue-lashing by Cindy, no gluteus-maximus vibrato by sweet Kathleen, what's a man to do?

Nothing but bourbon. And Mr. Mahler, now singing on solo flute, the dark secret bird of night. And my loaf of bread. Shall I call Mulligan? Lacey? Ferrigan? No, leave them in peace. Let them beings be.

Even the skin-show bars will be closing soon. Too late now for a heart to heart chat with Comfort and her swelling bosoms. (They're big, she says, but they're not very practical.) Or with golden-haired Sunshine and the tattooed butterfly on her thigh. Or Laura with the wicked and perjuring smile, and Whatshername and so on, they'll all be bolting off soon on the buddy seats of Harley choppers, each with one hand hooked in the waistband of the greasy bluejeans of her dope-dealing gun-smuggling child-molesting black-bearded beer-swilling pool-shooting ugly dirty evil old man. Bores and whores, all of them, but—fascinating. The smell of sin. That cockeyed coke-sniffing glister in the eyes. The smell of lust and money. The smell of salt, sweat, Listerine and sweet papaya juice. . .

Christ Jesus, don't think about it now. Trouble, nothing but trouble, trouble and danger and death in a ditch, you don't need that now. Glandular animals. Got to get off this wild stallion of desire before it carries me over a cliff, Pegasus without wings.

My bread has risen. Check the oven: 357° F. Good. I pop in the loaf and close the oven door, refill my glass and retreat to the easy chair in the living room, followed soon by the fragrance of baking bread. Even the smell makes me feel better.

Mahler explodes into his grand finale, vast heavenly choruses arching across the sky. An outburst of joy, clouds of exaltation piled on exaltation and then—a fierce short coda followed by silence. That golden stillness. "Silence always sounds good," said

Arnold Schonberg, explaining the odd pauses in *Pierrot Lunaire*. How true. Especially in the tortured, agonized, manacled music of Arnold Schonberg.

But my wife—?

Plainly, she is not coming back. I can tell by the pattern of cracks in the plaster. There's a code there, a message. Like the secret message in the final bars of Shostakovitch's 15th and last symphony. Faint cryptic signals, like the clicking of a telegraph key, against the remote and sustained monotone of the violins—a song from outer space. What was he trying to tell us? "I shall not return"? We'll never know.

But Elaine, how could she do this to me?

She has her reasons.

II

"Are you listening to me?"

I looked up from this book: Jaynes or somebody on the origin of consciousness or something. "What?"

"Are you listening to me?" she said.

"Yes. Sure. Of course."

"What did I say?"

"What?"

"What did I say?" Glaring at me.

"Well..." Trying to restore the unity of my broken-down bi-cameral mind, I stammered. "Well, honey, you said—what you always say." A limp evasion.

She laughed, not a pleasant laugh but a laugh of contempt, disgust, exasperation, defeat. "You never listen. Off in a world of your own. God I pity you, living in a world where nobody lives but you. What lousy company."

"I like it."

"You would. It's all you know." She shook the light brown hair from her eyes—those fine grave intelligent gray eyes, smoldering now with anger. Couldn't blame her one bit. Turned her eyes away, giving me the model's profile: the classic Nordic symmetry of vertical forehead, dark eyebrows, charcoal lashes emphasized with mascara, a short straight middleclass nose barely *retroussé* at the tip (the American touch), tiny nostrils, small but full-lipped mouth, delicate chin, the curving neck, these parts leading in turn to the chest with its high teenybopper titlets, the small and faintly convex belly, the narrow waist that I could almost clasp-around with my two hands. And then—but why go on with this tedious inventory? Everyone knows the formula. Why bother? Who cares?

Well now, we do care, don't we. Men care and women care because the men care. We're trapped in our biology, why not enjoy it? She was, in short, a trim little W.A.S.P.—white-Anglo-sexy-Protestant—not a perfect beauty by any means, but more or less the type the whole world now adores. Thanks to our planetary communications systems, magazines, movies, TV, video cassettes. Blonde hair, rosy skin, slender figure—why is it that men everywhere, from Fairbanks to Tierra del Fuego, from Oslo to Capetown, from Lisbon to Calcutta, yearn to clutch this creature in their arms? Two and a half billion mostly darkskinned blackhaired shortlegged men on the planet—and everyone, apparently, prefers a blonde? Including me. Why?

Who knows? Envy of the power and prestige of Europe and America? Some strange racial longing for the glow of the golden North, a hidden evolutionary drive toward this particular archetype? Are the angels, as we imagine, really honey-colored Honkies? The thought is too cruel to be borne. And very much *taboo*. But who can doubt it? Artificial female blondes swarm the streets of every nation—but where can you find girls naturally fair dying their hair black, wearing brown contact lenses, trying to widen their hips or shorten their legs?

It's not fair. Life is unfair and it's not fair that life is unfair. Is there no justice in the world? And no mercy neither? There is some but not much. No wonder they hate us down there in the lower hemisphere.

But as I was saying, she turned away from me, my fair Elaine. Finally. Finally gave up. No more argument, no more debate. I heard her packing a bag in the bedroom. A small one—she'd already moved most of her personal things to her boyfriend's place, Professor Schmuck, cybernetician. Seymour S. "Shithead" Schmuck. (Tomorrow I'll kill that guy. Tonight I'm baking bread.) Minutes later she was gone, slamming the door.

And was it my fault, another failed marriage? My second flop in the marital rodeo? The martial arts? Hard to say. I'm a nice man really. Not too bright, slow-witted, not very attentive—but well-meaning. You'd have to know me thoroughly to dislike me. My intentions are good.

"I love you, Henry," she'd say.

"You'll get over it, Elaine," I said, always kidding. And she did.

"You say you love me," she'd say, "but you don't show it." She was young, too young, only eighteen when I first clapped eyes— and then my hands—upon her. "You don't show it."

"What do you mean?" I said. "I'm crazy about you and you know it. Look at this thing."

"I don't mean that."

"Well what do you mean? I mean, Jesus Christ, I mean what do you want me to do? I mean, what do you *mean?*"

"I can't tell you. If you don't understand without me explaining everything there's no way I can tell you. I mean if I have to tell you you'll never understand."

"I see." My heart sank like lead beneath the weight of her imponderables, her incomprehensible phrases. I'd turn away and she'd turn away and I'd pick up a book or put on an Anton Bruckner or Tom T. Hall record or go for a ten mile walk in the moonlight or she would leave, slamming the door. Much to my immediate relief. I always loved the sound of my wife walking out the door, starting her Jap automobile, vanishing into the filthy city. To visit a friend? A relative? A relative friend? She was gone to visit her lover. And I never guessed or cared enough to guess. As long as she returned before morning I was content. I was a fool, but happy. Foolishly happy.

Longing for my Elaine, I plug in and telephone Kathleen. Lovely Kathleen. Lovely aroma of fresh bread in the kitchen. But who wants to break bread alone?

Yeah? She sounds sleepy. Kathy, it's me. It's late, Henry. I know, sweetheart, but I was thinking of you. I'll bet. I miss you.

You're drunk again. I'm a loving drunk. Oh, you're a loving man, always in love with somebody, you told me that once. I love you, Kathleen, desperately. Yeah, when you're desperate you love me. I want to tell you something. It's almost two, Henry; some of us have to go to work in the morning, you know. Tomorrow night? Maybe; maybe later. You still love me? I adore you. That's not what I asked. Have to go now, Henry. Wait a minute. Goodnight, Henry. . .

Click, followed by the electronic whine, as of cosmic mosquitos or background radiation, coursing through the circuits. Divine static. I detest that noise. I unplug the phone, just as it starts ringing, and open the oven door. My bread is ready, waiting for me. I grope for hotpads, pull out the pan, stagger to my feet using the stove for leverage, and empty the loaf from pan onto tabletop. Perfection. A hot firm shapely loaf, golden-brown, sweet as a virgin's haunch.

Breaking off the heel of the loaf, the best part, holding the warm and crusty chunk in my hand, I reach for the bottle of Wild Turkey, now almost empty, and slide down the wall to the kitchen floor. A bite of bread, a swallow of bourbon—God's on the job.

Nothing really helps. I should go for a long walk into the desert, take my agave stick, my pistol, our doomed dog, my jug of Gallo's Hearty Burgundy, fall in the gulch, finish the wine, shoot the dog, take a piss, vomit. That would help. Go to sleep on the cool sand while tarantulas creep on dainty hairy feet across my face, pausing to stare with sixteen compound eyes into the cavity of my ear. Then moving on, twitching a leg, to pastures new.

Courage. I crawl from kitchen into darkened living room,

feeling along the wall for the light switches, remove Mahler from the phonograph and install my hero the great American Charles Ives. An insurance executive, like Wallace Stevens, and our best composer yet. Symphony Number Four. At top volume, certainly: let the walls rock, the cinderblocks cringe, every nostril in the neighborhood bleed. I crawl for safety back to the kitchen under the terrific crashing chords of the opening—dual pianos in a black rage. A rage of rage! A dozen bars of thunder followed suddenly, quietly, by strange cloudy fantasies of mingled New England village bands, a fireman's parade, a churchly hymn, the ghost effects and haunted cemeteries full of Union dead. Nearer my God to thee, the chorus sings.

My great-great-uncle John Lightcap, half-starved P.O.W., escaped from Georgia's Libby Prison in 1863, spent two months sneaking homeward through Confederate territory living on goober peas, mushrooms, dandelion greens, arrived in Stump Crick West Virginia in time to learn that his son Elroy was dead, killed only a week before by bayonet at the battle of Gettysburg, 150 miles away. Pickett's last charge. Roy Lightcap's last stand. Uncle John's last war. "Haint' fightin' no more in Lincoln's dirty war," he said, resigning the captain's commission to which his men had elected him two years earlier. "He's so powerful strong on stompin' down the South and keepin' the Union big, let that cold-blooded murderous sonofabitch go down there to Georgia and fight his rotten war his own self. And take his coward son with him..."

Ives is my hero. A great musician, a great artist, and what is nearly as important, maybe more important, a great man.

Shakespeares and Mozarts and Marcel Prousts appear every century. Heroes are rare as radium.

Maybe I should see a psychiatrist. Two I've noted in the phonebook: Doctors Glasscock and Evilsizer. Or some kind of analyst: A barium enema, a proctoscopic probe. All-Bran and psyllium powder. The enema within. Join a Kundalini therapy group and take part in mystic oriental orgiastic rites. Write a book. Call it—*Cluster-Fuck: A Presbyterian Looks At Group Sex*. I may be the only redneck intellectual in America who's not yet been analyzed, psychoanalyzed, Rolfed, TMized, estered, sensory-deprived, reborn, spinologized or had my colon irrigated. Should get to know better those spiritual amphibia crawling in and out of Esalen hot tubs.

Once as a matter of fact I did let Elaine bully me into attending a group encounter session. She believed in it (that season) and felt that I needed it. My "hangups," she said, "bugged" her. E.g., my peculiar habit of shutting the bathroom door whan taking a crap. "Weird," she said, "far out," and paid $25 to get me in a group. I snuck out after ten minutes of holistic gender-blending, having enjoyed about as much as I could stand. All those warm fuzzies and fearless feelies massaging each others' emotional pudenda:

Who are you? says this man I never saw before, staring at me with the oversize, coterminous, pale eyes of a codfish. We sat on the floor facing each other, paired off like the others. For some reason there were no chairs in the room. Most of the group were knotted up in the lotus posture. Okay for bandy-legged little Asiatics but hard on a native American. I didn't even try it. All but me, I saw at a glance, were veterans of these rituals, very much at home, self-absorbed and comfortable. Everyone appeared to be less than forty years old. Another Lost Generation. We should've told them to Get Lost. And Stay Lost. (Now now, charity, charity...)

Who are you? he says again.

Who, me?

Who are you?

Well, the name's Lightcap. Henry H. Lightcap.

Who are you?

What?

Who are you?

I thought that's what you said. Who are *you?*

Who are you?

I get it. It's a game. Okay, who am I?

Who are you?

I looked around: the other pairs were doing the same, one asking Who are You? over and over, the other responding in some therapeutic manner. Only the session leader, a little hairy man from Topanga Canyon, California, was not taking direct part in the game. He lunged in a corner of the room supervising, a warm loving smile on his fried-veggie, overly suntanned face. Too many years spent staring into the sun, I suppose, trying to dissolve the old subject-object dichotomy that Descartes (they say) imposed on us. It's a "personal universe"; every window is really a mirror. (They say.) We are a bunch of windowless monads—nomads?— groping for return to the womb of total nullity, back to the flat world of bliss. But let's be open-minded about this.

Near the leader, leaning on the wall, was a bundle of foam-rubber bats; later these people would flog each other with the foam rubber, venting their angers in harmless futility. What good is that? Will only make them more furious in the long run. And two big bottles of massage oil. Oh no! Eight males, ten females, plus leader, and not a single pretty girl in the room. No wonder these folks are so testy. Beauty may be only skin deep but ugliness goes the whole way through.

But the leader looked pleased. He should. Since there were eighteen customers—patients? clients? students?—in the group, he'd just pocketed 18 x 25 dollars—$450 in legal tender. Not bad for one evening's work. Should be enough to pay for his first skin-cancer treatment. Bald-headed bushy-bearded fat-bellied little guru, no wonder he looked upon us with such warm regard. I saw him slip a glance at his wrist watch. He smiled when he caught me looking—a smile rich in beatitude, oozing with bliss, cool as a sunbeam in a cucumber. WE ARE ALL ONE, his T-shirt told me. That's a filthy lie, I thought, an insult to human potential.

Who are you? my partner kept chanting.

Who am I? I said. Who knows?

Who are you?

Why? I said. (He was getting perceptibly, if faintly, annoyed. My answers were wrong. I could see a trace of tension at the corners of his mouth.) Why who?

Who are you?

Who! I hooted like an owl. Who, who!

Who—(A tic in his left eyelid.)

Who who who!

—are—(A twitch on his lower lip.)

Who who who whoooooo, I concluded.

Fisheyes hesitated. He blinked several times. Who, he began again—

The group leader interrupted. Okay folks, time to switch. Now let your partner ask the Big Question. He checked his watch.

My opposite number relaxed. This part he liked. Hang loose, his manner said, keep cool and floppy-necked like a quiche-eater in a Naropa fern bar.

Okay, I says, so who are *you?*

He sighed, closing his large moist eyes. Who am I, he began— not a question but an overture. I am a mote in a sunlit pool, he said. I am a note in a symphony, dancing on the air. I am a photon of conscious light waltzing with electrons in the blue of the sky. He smiled.

That's a lie, I said.

Eyes closed, head tilted back, smiling through euphoria, he went on. I am a happy little neutrino in a cloud chamber, twinkling from quantum to quantum. I am a dancer with the Wu Li masters, floating through now and forever. I am a small idea in the great universal Mind.

I waited. His mouth opened then closed as I said, You're lying. You're a fish-faced grouper faking his way through a group encounter ripoff. You're a flatfoot floogie in a flimflam. You've been robbed of twenty-five dollars.

The itchy little tic reappeared in his left eyelid. Who am I, he sighed again, working hard to keep his cool lukewarm. I am a thought in the cosmic mind of Atman-Brahman. I am a molecule of organic energy on the ocean of eternity, evaporating happily toward the golden globe of ever-expanding space, finite but unbounded.

There's a piece of shit on your lower lip.

He frowned, reached toward his mouth, stopped, relaxed again, loose as a lily pad on a duck pond. Who am I, he chanted. I'm an attorney named Willis Butz—I mean, no, I'm, I'm nothing and I am everything, I am you and you am I and we are all one.

One what?

What?

One what?

He stopped. He opened his eyes. He glared at me. Who the hell *are* you, you bastard, and how'd you get in here?

I left. But not before recovering Elaine's $25 from the Head Fuzzy-Wuzzy. Give me my money back, I muttered in his ear, while the others were flailing backsides with their soft limp bats, or I'll make an ugly scene. The Guru frowned, mumbling something about no refunds. I'll tear this place apart, I said. He glanced around, smiling and nodding at the lambs who were watching us, then invited me to step outside for a minute. Expecting a karate attack, I followed carefully. In the hallway he said, Now what's your problem?

No problem. Just give back my $25.

You're a sick man, he said gently. You need help.

Give back that money, I said, or you'll need help. I mean medical help. I was bluffing, of course, but stood eight inches taller and outweighed him by twenty pounds. In the actual world, as opposed to the world of dancing Wu Li masters, bulk is important. I outbulked him—and would not be bilked. You're running a nasty little con-game here, I said, and you better be cautious. I should report you to the Better Business Bureau.

I do a lot for these people, he said sweetly. That's why they keep coming back.

If you helped them they wouldn't have to come back. They're a bunch of ageing adolescents and you're keeping them that way.

He looked up at me with soft empathic sympathetic eyes, out of that cooked-brown, wrinkled, fried and refried face. Do you realize that you are going through a midlife crisis?

Not only me, I said. The whole world is going through a midlife crisis. I held out my hand. The twenty-five.

The world is an illusion.

I know. But it's a real illusion, the only one we got. The money, please.

He returned my money. You big shit, he said over his shoulder as he walked away.

I didn't argue. Let the poor fakir have the last word, what the hell. Is that not the latest wisdom from Swami-Roshi-Yogi-rambananabung? Sure it is. Every man his own guru, I thought, every lady her own gurette.

Laughing all the way to the Dirty Shame Saloon where I found myself among friends—Mulligan, Lacey, Arriaga and Harrington. I want to buy a drink, I said, for every man in the house, if any. When Elaine's $25 was gone I drove home at a slow, safe, sedated pace, unnoticed by the "authorities," threw up in the driveway, crept into the house on hands and knees as a devout brain-retreaded pilgrim should, and fumbled around for the light switch. I knew it was somewhere on the wall. But where was the wall?

The lights blazed on.

She glared at me. Her turn now. You bastard! she said. (That word again.) And started to cry. It took half an hour of my wormiest cajolery before I could wrap her in my lawful loving conjugal arms, thirty minutes more until we became one flesh.

But what sweet, succulent, soothing flesh.

Elaine...

III

Actually I'm thinking of Kathleen again. That too was part of the problem. As I stepped from the shower, towelling my wet head, dripping over her bathroom rug, she was waiting for me on her knees, head high to my groin. At once she took my flaccid tool in her mouth and sucked on it thoughtfully, like a child with a lollipop. "Jesus christ, Kathy, wait a minute—" But she knew what she was doing, she knew the way to a man's heart. I did not love her, as such sentiments are understood, but I sure was fond of her. And growing fonder by the moment. I've never met a nymphomaniac I didn't like.

She drew back her head and gazed with pride at what she had done to me. What hath God wrought.

"It's huge," she said. "Terrifying. An enormous engine of power and lust." Kathleen, I'm sorry to say, was an eager reader of fake Victorian novels by "Anon," and the more erotic women's romance novels. She loved gaslight theater and longed to be an actress. She admired Erica Jong (alas!) and the male dong or what she called the 20-centimeter peter.

I stepped on her bathroom scale. We looked at the pointer. "Kathy, you made me gain five pounds."

She resumed her work. I dropped the towel—it caught and hung on my erection—and drew her up, kissed her. She nibbled on my upper lip, then the lower. There was a faint flavor of Herbal Essence on her tongue. I picked her up and carried her, slung like a cat in my arms, to the one real room of her "studio" apartment and draped her, belly down, over the back of the sofa. I raised the skirt of her nightie and contemplated the roundest, rosiest, liveliest rear-end in Tucson. To the best of my knowledge. She squealed in mock terror and flexed that thing, making it tremble like a frightened bivalve. Must be jelly, I thought, jam don't shake like that. The most *eloquent* ass I've ever been privileged to know, socially. And she knew it.

Lost in reverence, I rested my friendly weapon for a moment in the crease of her glowing buttocks. Under my cool hands they felt like warm sun-ripened melons. Honeydew melons. *(Claire!)*

"Please sir," she begged, "do not attempt to thrust that hard thick huge enormous engine of yours up into my tight tiny pussy by force."

"Why not?"

"It's too huge."

I said, "You're probably right, Miss Kathy. But let's give it a try."

She groaned, quivered, buried her face in the pillows. Embroidered by her mother. "Please sir, I'm only a helpless maid," came her muffled voice. She loved to play this role. "A virgin girl."

"Well I'm the Sardar of Samarkand," I said, smacking her across the cheeks. "Spread your legs."

"Oh please sir—"

Whack! (Remember the Koranic injunction to woman: Keep a still tongue in thy head but scream with pleasure when he mounts thee.) She parted her thighs, revealing the sacred groove, the holy grot, the shrine of the ages. For a moment, silent, I pondered the mystical rose, moist with dew. Pretty—but is it art?

She stirred, twitching one buttock then the other. "Do you like me, sir?" She raised her hips, trying to capture my rod with her labia majorem, to pull it into the aching cavity of inner space. Her inner tube. Or so I surmised. Vita brevis, ars longa. Long enough, anyhow. I trained the cocked torpedo on the vaginal entrance, shut my eyes and plunged in to the hilt, a typical quarterback sneak. She groaned, moaned, shivered like a dog in the rain and clamped herself around me with the grip of a suction cup. The hungry clam.

We will now have a brief intromission...

IV

That helps some but not much. I am alone in my kitchen again, cooling fast, me and my minor puddle of passion on the linoleum tiles. Self abuse—God's one great gift to the lonely man—has let me down again, spent but not satisfied, lonelier than before.

I gnaw my crust, inhale the fumes from an empty bottle. She loved me, did she not? Elaine, I mean. Nearly three years together, through the better and the worse. It seemed much longer. And now, suddenly, she is gone. I feel her absence as a tangible, living, palpable presence. But when I look—she is not here. Where she was is nothing. The void. A psychic amputation.

Henry raises his dark head, sees himself reflected in the black night glass of the window. Deux Henri! A homely man with black oily hair, beak of a nose, jaw like a two-by-four. He grins his evil wolfish grin. Nobody so wicked in appearance could feel such pain, right? Stands to reason. But he does and the face fades out, obliterated by ennui, leaving the empty moronic grin which fades in turn.

He howls softly like a dog and beats his forepaws on the floor. That helps a little. Not really. There is no remedy. Oh Death thou comest when I had thee least in mind. Winter in the heart. Antarctica in my soul.

He senses within his head an avalanche of whisky-sodden brain cells losing their purchase on stability, sliding like a Malibu mudbank into the landfill of his cerebellum. Whole tiers and galleries of corrupted gray matter fall with a CRASH! into the sinkhole of his spirit.

He thinks of the cheap panelling above the urinal in a bikers' bar on Speedway. On that wall where the graffiti are inscribed with knife blades, some condemned soul in the fraternity of the damned had written

No chance.

No hope.

No escape.

So what. What of it. Keep sliding, let it fall, somewhere down in here we'll hit bottom, reach bedrock, and bottom out. And then, like this honest loaf in my hand, we'll rise again. Villon says,

Mort, j'appelle de ta rigueur...

Death, I challenge you to do your worst, you who ravished my

Death, I challenge you to do your worst, you who ravished my mistress, stole her from me and will not be satisfied until you have me too in your clutches. Yes, Death, I challenge you to do your worst. You're called. Let's see your hand.

According to the latest micro-biologists my body is really nothing but a megalopolis of unicellular organisms. According to the theories of the chief witch doctors of the *new* physics (now about 85 years old) we and our sweethearts, our women, our children, our friends, our pet dogs, are "really" nothing "but" a whirligig system of swarming sub-atomic events, ephemeral as Mayflies on a breezy day in spring.

Is that so. You don't say.

Ignore them. They haven't got Henry Lightcap in a circuitron or under their electron microscopes yet—and they never will. The world is bigger than those metaphysical black-hole sphincters will ever understand. One man—with a woman in his arms— outweighs their whole slimey universe of nuclear ectoplasm, graph-paper abstractions and Day-Glo polka-dot electric Kool-ade scientific pointillism.

That's what I think and my name is Henry Lightcap. Henry H. Lightcap. Henry Holyoak Lightcap, by Christ and by damn.

Jesus, this bottle is empty. My bread is cold. There is no woman in my arms. Take another piece of bread, Henry, and think of something. Of what? Of something. Think of—

Alicia. Melanie. Melody. Gertrude. The prettiest girl I ever knew was named Myrtle Dieffendeffer. The second prettiest was Eleanor Barff. How about—Caroline? Lola? Birgit? Bridget? Candace? Candace—ah yes, Candy. Who could forget Candy? Or

How I Got Pseudo-Pleurisy On My Summer Vacation While
Making Love to Candy once on the ground and twice on the
tailgate of a pickup truck during a hailstorm on Dead Horse Point,
Utah after running through the rain, smoking two joints and
drinking three sixpacks of Old Milwaukee (Walgreen's special) in
the effort to drown a hangover from the night before.

Demerol? Percodan? One thinks of heavy sedation at a time
like this. .357? A .44 magnum? Should go gunning for Dr. and
Mrs. Schmuck. Load the old 12-gauge, one barrel for each, a crime
of passion. No decent jury would convict. They'd be weeping
throughout the Public Defender's summation. "Manslaughter," at
worst. Maybe "negligent homicide." Get my picture in the papers.
Be a hero, swamped with hand-penned letters from lovesick
females. Phone ringing like a burglar alarm with calls from ladies
sick for love.

It's no help. Think, Henry, think.

He grins the grin. Keels forward on his face, thinking: I've got
to see Will. Got to get to Will's. There just hain't no alternative.
But God—three fucking thousand five hundred fucking miles east
of the Santa Cruz River. Too far. 3500 miles!

Will, why ain't you here?

V

Where am I now? (Panic.)

Black in here as a witch's womb.

He rises to hands and knees, feels along wall for light switch.
Click. No light (Terror.) Maybe I'm dead. Dark as a tomb in here.

Try switch again. Still no light. That's right, the bulb, never did change that bulb. My God for a minute I thought I'd gone blind. Or died. But where am I anyway? Which bulb? Last time I looked I was in the kitchen eating bread by the light of the oven, remembering Kathleen, recalling Candy, missing Elaine.

He listens. The house seems strangely quiet. Then remembers—the Frigidaire is dead. Shot in the bowels and left for junk. He gropes forward, feels the picture-window draperies in his hand and pulls, hauling himself to his feet. The drapes come down and he falls with them, stumbling over one of Elaine's footstools, endtables, tablelamps, coffeetables, piano benches, something. On his knees again.

Good sweet Christ, he prays.

But he has succeeded at least in admitting light to the room. Through the window he sees a multitude of lights—a city—and over the eastern mountains the eerie red glow of one more cloudless dawn. A false dawn? Perhaps. One never knows. But where? What city? What world is this?

"Elaine," I call. No answer. "Elaine?"

At once the sick despair rises in my veins like an injection of some lethal drug. Like an overdose of lithium. To hell with that. I'll not yield this time. It's a new day a-dawning. It's the new Henry Lightcap here, on hands and knees, tongue hanging out like a technicolored necktie, and we're fighting it this time, boy, I tell you boy no little woman is a-gonna keep Henry Lightcap down for long. Not Henry *H.* Lightcap.

Lightcap rising with the morn. I hear a cactus wren chatter outside in the cholla thickets, the sharp clear whistle of a curvebill thrasher, the lonesome peep of a phainopepla, the true song of a cardinal or maybe it's a mockingbird. And my name is Ivan Ilyich, by God, and I'm crawling up from the dead. Lazarus returns. This here is Lightcap speaking, men, and it takes more than a woman, more than a quart of Wild Turkey, more than another routine marital disaster, more than one more standard moral catastrophe, to keep old Henry down.

I stand up on my two feet like a man.

Something cold hangs from my open fly, limp, long, lonely as a snake. I tuck it back in and zip up. Let us have—music! Coffee! Sausage and eggs! Time for the quick emotional lift, then the caffeine, then the basic American grease fix.

A gray light fills the room, dim but good enough to see by. Music first. I sit on the shaky bench before our old-time cabinet grand and stare at the keys. Eighty-eight keys that open the door to a nicer world than this. I lift my hands, straighten my back, and hammer out—fortissimo—five great six-fingered Lightcapian chords: C minor, F-sharp minor, G major, C major, E-flat major! Resurrection! Bare foot heavy on the petal, I recapitulate, then launch into wild improvisation. A splendid massive cloud of sound rises from the piano. I learned this technique from Charles Ives, nobody else. Keep that right-foot on the pedal and when the cacophony seems unendurable pour on more coal, more power, more glory.

Crashing up and down the keyboard like a lion crushing cane, like a stallion trampling Fritos, like an elephant in bamboo, like a bull stomping crockery, like a turkey through the corn—Dubarry done gone again!—I modulate suddenly, with wrenching force, into the finale of Schubert's "Unfinished Symphony," then Beethoven's 5th, then Bruckner's 5th, Mahler's 5th, Tschaikowsky's 5th, the Sibelius 5th, Carl Nielsen's 5th, the Prokofiev 5th (a mad socialist industrial machine running amok), the Shostakovitch 5th, and finally, naturally, old Johannes Brahms his 5th.

Leaving the ducal grand salon, his cigar smoking like a chimney, Brahms said in farewell to the assembled lords and ladies, "If there's anyone here I've failed to insult—I apologize." Good man. A born-again atheist in more ways than one.

Brahms never wrote a 5th Symphony, the nitpickers will object. Nor Schubert a *finale* to his 7th. Well they have now. I wrote it for them and it may well be their finest work. It is fact, curious but true, that most symphonists reach apogee, produce their liveliest most vigorous most dramatic work (not necessarily their *best*), in their fifth effort.

And women? Who will write the first great women's 5th? I will. I'll do it for them. Nobody's gonna call Henry Lightcap a sexist pig, not around here they don't.

Enough of this esoterica; time for the coffee and the grease. I put a Schutz motet and a Merle Haggard song-cycle on the music machine and head for the kitchen, followed by the golden vapor of Schutz's angelic, medieval, divine, choral harmonics. Set kettle on burner, stick filter in Pyrex jug, pat sausage into patties and put skillet on stove. Smell them nitrates sizzle—good!

I take four eggs from the silent, bullet-stricken refrigerator— warm and damp in there—and look about for a clean bowl. Sink crowded with dirty dishes, pots, pans, wineglasses, tumblers, bowls, garbage. But there's Elaine's *wok*—walk? woke?—hanging on the wall. That will do. I crack the eggs, dump in a canfull of El Pato's diced green chiles, and stir the steaming mess with a wooden spoon, creating out of chaos a rational, systemic paradigm of order. Scrambled entropy, edible.

The miracle of eggs. In the beginning was the egg. The chicken was an afterthought, a mere transmission mechanism for the production of further eggs. The world itself is egg-like. Those astro-photos of galaxies, spiral nebulae—do they not resemble fresh eggs broken in the pan? The universe itself may be no more than one gigantic cosmic egg. And the function of mind? To fertilize that egg. Creating—who knows what grotesque and God-like monster. Best not think about it.

Stirring my eggs in her wok, I recall Elaine's artistic cooking period. She was a fad follower, like most of us, straining to keep up with the latest fashion, always a shade behind. Est and Arica, group encounter therapy, aerobic dancing, jogging, haute cuisine, cuisine minceur, primal screaming, Zen, John Anderson, Gloria Steinem, fat-tire bicycles, punk rock, acid rock, acid rain, Elton John, Bill Marley and the Rastafarians, Back to the Bible, soap opera, home computers, Bucky Fuller and geodesic domes, whole Earth Catalogs and polka-dot physics, whatever the thing of the week, the trend of the month, the rage of the season, she was onto it like a leach, into it like a chigger. And so for a time—maybe a month—early in our marriage, she turned her nervous but insecure temperament and incoherent energies toward the high art of *cuisine francaise*.

How can I forget the day she tried to serve me *oeuf poché en aspic*. Surely one of the most repellent inventions in all of human

history. Frogs and viscosity. "France," said Henri de Montherlant
(a good Frenchman), "is the woman of Europe." That was when
our troubles began, was it not?

"What's this?" I said.

"Poached egg in aspic," she said. There was a blush of pride on
her sweet rosy Saxon face. Her violet eyes glowed like industrial-
strength sapphires.

"Aspic? It looks like—like. . ." Like something out of a horse's
hoof, I thought but did not say aloud.

"It's a tomato sauce gel," she said. "A kind of gelatin." She was
watching me closely, insecure and already nervous. "It's good,
Henry." She ate a spoonful; I watched in horror. "Please Henry.
It's very good. Really." She probed deeper with her silver spoon (a
gift from her Grandmaw Hutchins) and broke the soft egg inside.
A yellowish foetus-amoeba spread within the menstrual-colored
jelly. To me it resembled something out of a nightmare by Poe.
The facts in the case of V. Waldemar.

Under Elaine's watchful eye, I took my spoon and touched the
thing on my plate. It quivered as if still alive. "Elaine," I said,
"you're my darling and I love you, urgently, more than life itself,
and I know this must have taken great time and effort. . ."

She stared at me. I knew she was going to cry.

". . .and I really appreciate this, honey, but doggone it sweetheart I was outside all day in the cold and the wind [I'd been out
bow-hunting with Lacey] and you know I'm kind of really hungry.
I mean hungry. Can't we—do you think maybe—I mean, could I
maybe *fry* this hideous thing?"

She rose from the table.

"I didn't mean that," I said at once, "didn't mean that, only kidding, darling, look, watch, I'm going to eat it. Watch." Too late. She groped toward the bedroom, blind with tears. Me and my big loose mouth. "Honey," I shouted, "you know I'm only kidding, honey." I got up from my chair. "Elaine!" I roared as the bedroom door slammed in my face.

She was a master—a mistress—at slamming doors. One of her favorite gestures. Every doorframe in the house is outlined with ornamental traceries of cracked plaster. I could hear her sobbing inside, that awful hoarse asthmatic weeping. Too many cigarettes in her teenybopper years. I tried the door but she had turned the key in the lock.

Useless for me to hammer on the door or to attempt, prematurely, the first necessary signals toward reconciliation. I returned to our "dining nook" in the kitchen, in this tract-style travesty of a house, and looked again at the blob of inedible pink matter on my plate. That glob of misery and mystery. I set it on the floor in front of Fred the cat. He sniffed cautiously, not quite touching it, and backed off. I took the plate outside and offered the thing to Solstice our dog. (Born on June 22nd.) She didn't want it either. So I flung it, plate and all, into the branches of the chinaberry tree in our frontyard. The living glop oozed down from twig to twig in mucusoid hockers, like snot from a sick calf, and dropped onto the defenseless pads of a prickly pear. There it gathered itself together again, coagulating on the spines, and continued its slimy progress toward the center of the earth.

Back in the kitchen I fried myself a pound of pigmeat and four eggs, over hard. Galvanized. When Elaine finally emerged from the bedroom I told her I'd eaten the egg-in-aspic but was still a mite famished, thus the reek of bacon on the air. She knew I was lying.

That was near the end of the honeymoon, the typical ninety days of passion before the grim reality of domestic bliss begins to sink into the mutual consciousness of man and wife. It was only the first of many such incidents. One evening when I came home from work she greeted me at the door wearing a brocaded kimono.

Beautiful, I said. She smiled, bowed, led me inside. Supper was ready. But it was on the floor—or more precisely, laid out upon this foot-high endtable. Barely off the floor. I sat down, Elaine pulled off my boots, washed my hands with warm rose-water in a porcelain bowl. She knelt on a cushion at one side of the low table, I knelt on a cushion opposite.

But this position was uncomfortable for me. I changed to a sitting posture but there was no room for my legs—I'm 6′ 4″— either in front of, beside or beneath that damnable toy table. Nor did I have anything to lean back against. I placed my cushion back further so that I could recline against the front of the sofa. But then I could not reach the table. I pulled the endtable closer, across the carpet, and toppled a slender vase filled with fresh live— chrysanthemums? Oh damn! I'm sorry, Elaine.

She smiled and said nothing, sopped up the water with a napkin, replaced the flowers. Smiling graciously, she poured the tea, an authentic Chinese brew called Soochang Bing—or Bong, I believe. The kind that tastes and smells like mildewed straw soaked for six months in a horse trough. Delicious, I said, closing my eyes the better to savor the rare bouquet of the tea. (Quelle bouquet!)

She smiled, eyes lowered, removed the lid from a porcelain pot and with matching ladle served a dark thick purple soup into tiny porcelain soupbowls. A tincture of iodine hovered on the air. We picked up miniature matching scoop-like spoons. The spoons were too short to sup from at the side, too thick and awkwardly curved to allow insertion into the mouth. The idea, evidently, is to bend the head far back and pour contents of spoon into mouth, as if feeding an infant.

I worked on it and got a few mouthfuls down. Best boiled sewage effluent I ever tasted. Elaine observing my every move, each response, with hopeful eyes. Well? she asked, as I paused for reflection. Good, I said, good, mighty good, what is it? It's a sort of Japanese bouillabaisse, she said, called Maru Tamayaki. If I heard her correctly. Really good, I said, wondering what kind of marine life was in the soup but afraid to ask.

I dipped my scoop deeper into my little bowl and came up with something dead white, a languid soft invertebrate substance. Testicles of octopus? Placenta of jellyfish? What's this? I said. Tofu, she said; soybean curd. Soybean *curd?* Come on, Henry, you've heard of tofu, stop pretending to be so—plebian; it's good and it's very nutritious, it's a staple of the Japanese diet, you'll like it. She swallowed a spoonful of the stuff and watched me.

I smiled at my wife and placed the wet tofu in my mouth, swallowing quickly before I lost courage. It went down easily enough, I guess, although I felt a queasy tremor of protest from my stomach. Delicious! I exclaimed.

I knew you'd like it.

Tofu, eh? Those Orientals sure are clever little fuckers. I groped for another lucky dip, feeling about for some sort of solid muck. Soybean mash, I was thinking—in America we make cattle eat it. No wonder there's so many short people on this planet. I groped in the opaque, beet-dark soup and fished up maybe a dying squid—limp strands of purple pseudo-flesh dangling like tentacles from my spoon. I looked at Elaine; she was watching.

Kelp, she explained.

Kelp?

Kelp. You know what kelp is.

You mean—seaweed?

Yes. The tears (goddamn it) already welling to the surface of those marvelous eyes. Please don't be so suspicious, Henry. I'm not trying to poison you or anything, you know.

I know, honey, really, it looks good. Real good. I was just curious, honest. Just never saw anything like this before crawling in my soup.

She stiffened.

So it's kelp? I went on hastily, kelp, eh? Well I'll be damned. Wonderful. Amazing. I stared at the thing hanging from my spoon, not quite brave enough to bring it to my lips. Like the innocent North Dakota virgin who married a Frenchman and wondered, after five years of steady sex, why she never got pregnant, I could not quite bring myself to swallow the stuff. I knew I could not get it down.

Those little Nips are an ingenious people, I said. Sony, Datsun, Toyota, Kawasaki, Honda, sepuku, kamikaze, hari-kari, Pearl

Harbor, the creeping kudzu vine—how can we ever thank them? And now kelp, seaweed in my soup, what do you know about that. Wonderful. Well, with a hundred million of the little brown mothers crammed onto a few islands barely big enough for maybe one half million actual humans, no wonder they have to eat seaweed. And soybean curd, whales, krill, birds' nests, labels off beer bottles.

Birds' nest soup is a Chinese dish.

One billion of *them.* Eat more beef, I say.

Now she was getting angry. Her High Church blood was flowing. If we Americans didn't feed so much grain to cattle and hogs, we could support millions of people. Billions. Africa, Asia, Latin America, we could feed them all.

There's too many short people in this world already. Far too many. Beat them down, I say, down, with vigorous blows about the head and shoulders.

You're talking like an idiot. You don't really believe that height makes you superior. A pause. Do you?

I shrugged. Yes and no. Put it this way: if those billions of short people are as good as us, why do they have such small heads?

You're sick. You and Hitler should get together. You'd love South Africa. Why don't you join the KKK? Silence. She watched me still looking at the Oriental weed hanging from my spoon. Well—are you going to eat it or not?

Elaine... I looked at her. Her eyes were wet with tears. Lower lip a-tremble. Elaine, sweetheart, I was born and bred on a sidehill farm in Appalachia. Actually bred first, then born. Hain't we got no taters? pokeweed greens? turnips? smoked ham? redeye gravy?

sweetcorn? sowbelly? venison sausage? or even beans? And I mean beans, not bean sprouts.

You were born in a barn. More likely a pigsty.

Our Lord & Savior was born in a barn, I reminded her. I recited my favorite Christian poem:

> There was an old bugger named God
> Who put a young virgin in prod
> This amazing behavior
> Gave us Jesus our Savior
> Who died on a cross, the poor slob.

Elaine put down bowl and spoon. False rhyme, she said. Daintily she dabbed her lips with napkin. She was making a patient effort to control herself, her rage, her anguish. Gracefully she started to rise—

I gulped down the mass of soggy kelp. Half choking I croaked, "Good, honey, goddamn it's good. Damn good. Delectable. My Christ but it's good. I mean quite fucking superb."

But I was late, too late with too little. Tears streaming down her pink glossy cheeks, she bolted for the bedroom.

"Elaine!" I howled. Too late again. The door slammed shut. The lock snapped to. The dreadful racked weeping sounded through the hallway.

Too late the phalarope. Grabbing the bottle of saki, which tastes no worse than Gallo's hearty chablis, I got up, got out, drove to the Raunchhouse Bar & Grill, ordered a hot turkey sandwich with mashed potatoes, gravy, cranberry sauce and Green Giant corn niblets. (The waiter brought the can itself for my inspection, as customary in a high class place, showed me the label, and with due ceremony and graceful flourishes pulled an opener from his belt and opened the can right there, at the table, in my presence, as etiquette requires.) I washed the meal down with three bottles of Budweiser topped off with a Dutch Masters cigar, Walgreen's best. Satisfied, I asked myself a question:

Lightcap, How can you be so rotten? How can you be such a rotten obnoxious swine? Which I answered with the only possible answer, It ain't easy.

* * *

And then there was the *quiche Elaine*.

"What's this?"

"Quiche of course."

"Keesh? *Keesh?*"

"Of course."

This was a cheesy pudding inset with greenish fragments of spinach or asparagus, baked in a good decent piecrust which could have been used for rabbit or squirrel or iguana, for Christ's sake. "Well, keesh, is it? Some kind of Arab dish?" (It looked like something A-rabs would eat.) I was thinking of *kef* and other derivatives of hashish.

"It's French, as you well know." She spelled it out for me.

"Ah ha! Quiche. Mais oui. Looks lovely, honey." I buttered a chunk of bread, my own homebaked honest wholegrain wheat-berry wonderbread, staff and stuff of life, true soul food, and waited as Elaine cut the quiche into pie-shaped sections and served me one. I took a dainty forkful between my mandibles. She poured a chilled Moselle into our wine-glasses, watching me like a redtail hawk on a telephone pole. The quiche tasted vaguely like...like vague...rather like vagueness itself. Bland as blancmange— another typical Frog dish. Not bad, not good, but at least edible. A nice cheese flavor. I liked the piecrust.

Pleased, I took a second bite and gulped it down, then drank the wine. I hate white wine—to me all white wine tastes like unleaded angel piss. But what the hell. I was determined that this time I would not fail her. I ate a third bite of the cheesy suet. And another.

Smiling her forced, bright smile, she said, "Well?"

I swallowed. "Delicious..." I drank more of the wine, took a hearty bite from my chunk of bread. "Very good, sweetheart. Really good."

"Don't sweetheart me, you don't like it, do you?"

"It's great." Hurriedly I forked up another gobbet of the quiche Elaine. "Great stuff."

"Oh what a liar." Tears starting up again, she left the table in a hurry, knocking over the wine bottle. I restored the bottle to an upright posture, quickly. Wine is wine. I ran after her, begging forgiveness. Too late. Another evening of connubial tranquility blown into the air, lost forever, flipped away like shit off a shingle. Careless love.

The marriage lasted two years despite her experiment with gourmet cooking. What actually wrecked our permanent relationship, permanently, was the usual thing, namely love. L'amore, el amor, l'amour, das Liebe, sexual love, that traditional incommensurable in the male-female relationship. Some ship it is, too. Leaky as an unstaunched wench, as Shakespeare said.

How can I be true to one, wrote Byron, without being false to all the others? Precisely. Precisely my difficulty. It's not that I wanted them all—as pointed out before I'm no sexist pig—but I did want all the ones I wanted.

Why? What made me this way? I know why I love sexy girls, lovely women—but why do I love them so much? Am I queer? Where did I go wrong? What is this thing called love? ("A gentle knight was pricking on the plain...")

Put it this way: I've always been the servant of my cock. That prong dong pizzle prick dick whanger banger rod staff pike pen pencil sword gun trigger ram joystick joyprong love-bone dipstick, combination tool, whatever they call it these days.

Can't seem to get over my fondness for this instrument— always fondling it. Following wherever it leads. Whither thou goest I shall go. Blind faith, blind devotion. Love is blind. This pseudo-pod, this prehensile penis, this extensible scimitar of flesh, this thing like the nose of a possum forever sniffing out tender pudenda in pastures new.

Paradise, say the Arabs, begins one hand's-breadth south of a pretty girl's sash. Three principal charms hath a new mistress, the French say: The first is beauty, the second gentleness, the third novelty; and the greatest of these is novelty.

Lust is not love, say the critics. But where does one end and the other begin? Lust leads to love as sure as adventure leads to trouble. For friendship a man prefers a man, for love he needs a woman.

As for the needs of woman, what man can say? Woman is a different world, a different race, another species, so deeply

radically permanently different from men it's a miracle we can
interbreed with them. Or that they permit it. But as we all know
it's precisely that dramatic difference which creates the interest—
the tension and the delight.

Down with unisex. Death to all androgynes.

It took me only a couple of months to cure Elaine of gourmet
cookery. We went back to basic American fare—the pig and the
egg for breakfast, the cheese and crackers and tuna for lunch, the
cow and chicken and lamb for supper. With mashed potatoes and
gravy, with turnips and blackeye peas, with beer and red wine. A
good diet for me, I was working outside in the open air in those
days, at the wildlife reserve, but poor Elaine began to put on
weight in the thigh and hip. That did not trouble me; I liked her
plump, well-rounded; but she, like millions of other females here
and abroad, had been trained to believe she must have the flanks
of a whippet, the buttocks of a boy. Hated androgyny again! She
trimmed her diet down to salads and yoghurts while her husband
carved his protein and chomped on carbohydrates. She became a
jogger.

No!

What's it to you, gorebelly. (She was an English major that
term. Welding and auto mechanics the next year with a minor in
gymnastic dance. Computer science the following year.)

She bought the uniform: the Nike shoes, the flimsy erotic
Adida track shorts, the heavy-duty reinforced breast sling, the
long-billed sunshade, even the headset FM/AM Walkman radio,
and commenced to laboring up and down the streets with Eric
Clapton and James Taylor bawling in her ears, the jogger's look of

smug pain and spiritual fortitude on her face. Favoring her sore foot, she gulped the dust and grime and noxious gases of the passing motor traffic.

Conserve energy, I pleaded. Running is wasteful. All joggers should be chained to treadmills and compelled, under whiplash, to generate electricity.

Bug off.

I'll buy you a new ax. A maul. Wedges. A sledge hammer. We need more firewood. More rocks for the garden wall.

Drop dead.

I dropped the subject.

The euphoria of running wore off after she'd dropped five pounds and gained a shin splint and two bulging calf muscles. Next move? I braced myself.

Feminism reared its fearsome head, a fright wig crawling with serpents, eyes to paralyze Achilles, the grievance of a million years of servitude glaring from the dark recesses of the female mind.

She came under evil influence at the University, as I should have anticipated. Led astray by bad companions, she began reading Woolf, Greer, Friedan, Steinem, Beauvoir, Firestone, Millet, Schulman, Brownmiller, Rich and other restless Hebraic natives from the rubyfruit jungle. A school of hagfish. Virginia Woolf had suddenly become—that very year—one of the world's great writers. But not Jane Austen: Austen condones marriage, even urges its pursuit as a legitimate option for upwardly-mobile bourgeois-type girls. What was Jane Austen ever interested in *but* marriage? Furthermore Austen had refused to be born Jewish and who but the Semites, from Moses and Jesus and Paul and

Mahomet to Freud and Ayatollah Khomeni, have succeeded in making of sex so gruesome a rack of torture? Five hundred million decapitated foreskins. Half a billion vaginas dentata. Who's afraid of Virginia Woolf? Me—I am.

Combat in the errogenous zone. The "Joy" of Sex—the S. Hite or Shite Report. Oh, shit . . .

VI

I was dozing off to sleep one night, deplete and satisfied after a brisk little bout in bed with Elaine, when she muttered these curious words in my ear:

"We're going to change that old format."

"Pardon?"

"Change that old format."

"Sure, honey . . ." My heavy lids dropped down again. I was a happy man, ready for the blissful dreams that follow spendthrift sperm. What's this post-coitus regret bullshit? In the sweet hiatus after sexual love I tend to hear little thrushes calling from magnolia trees in Paradise. ("Paradise"—another word for man's original garden: the wilderness.) After making love I feel not sadness but serenity, hear bluebirds in an alpine meadow, dream mystical daydreams in the out-of-doors.

But I was attacked by an unkindness of ravens. Not a dissimulation of birds or exaltation of larks but a gaggle of geese, a murder of crows, a coven of witches:

"Did you hear me, Henry?"

"What?"

"Did you hear me?"

"Sure, honey, you bet."

"What did I say?"

I struggled against my drowsiness, sensing danger. "You said, did I hear you."

"Yes. And what did I say?"

I thought. Thought hard, mastering my irritation. Irritation? Homicidal outrage: there's nothing I hate more than being disturbed during those exquisitely languorous moments when drifting into slumber. And I have a bad temper, though I'm fighting it. I said, "You said, Did you hear me."

She gritted her fine sharp teeth. In an icy voice, teeth like icicles, she said, "I said we're going to change that old format."

"What old format?"

"Foreplay, penetration, ejaculation, sleep," she recited, as if it were a formula.

"What's wrong with it?"

"It's no good. It's obsolete."

Ominous word. I tried to be helpful. "We could skip the foreplay."

"I'm serious."

"Save the foreplay for later."

"Henry, a woman has needs too, you know. We're serious."

We? Another ominous word. "We? Who's we, white woman?"

"You know what I mean." She was tense, frigid with anger, at the same time slightly fearful. This was a new sensation for her, baiting her man.

"No, I don't know what *we* mean." Temper, temper. "I mean

what you mean. What do you mean? You're talking about coming?
going? unloading rocks? the big round O? the holy tortilla?"

She started to rise from bed. "I'm leaving."

I grabbed her. "Why are you always threatening to leave? Is
that the only way you can carry on a discussion?" (Here's your hat,
there's the door, what's your hurry?) "You mean you didn't come
this time, is that what you're mad about?"

"You know."

"Know what?"

"What you said. Yes, I did not—come. As you so crudely put it."

"Oh? Crude? You didn't come?" (And I thought I'd put it very
nicely, tactfully, as I always put it.)

"Henry—I never come."

Pause. Silence. The words sink.

"Oh God," I said. (I'm going to write a book someday: *The Joy
of Jerking Off*. At least you don't have to talk afterwards.) "What
the hell do you mean you never come. *Never?* Hardly ever?"

"I mean never, Henry. You know what never means."

"Forever?"

"Never. Not yet."

"I can't believe this, Elaine. What the hell do you mean?" Now
I was getting irked, rising to my elbows, another good night's
sleep ruined, nothing for it now but aspirin, Wild Turkey, hours of
Gibbon or Burton or Shakespeare under the reading lamp and
that feeling by dawn of total moral and mortal exhaustion. I'm
going to write a book. "We've been officially married two years,
Elaine. Sleeping together, fucking together, fighting together for
over three years and now you claim you never come. Never came?
Never? Not once?"

"Fight and fuck," she said. "fuck and fight, that's all we ever do."

"What's wrong with that? That's better than most people have it." Pause. "Not even once? In three whole years?"

"Not once."

"You've been faking all this time? All that groaning and gasping and clasping and wiggling, that was a fake?"

"You're the fake."

"My God, Elaine, I can't believe it. I can't believe this."

"It's true."

"Oh, God. . ." I was in trouble. "Is it my fault?" Silence. Pregnant silence. "What about—other men?"

She hesitated in what I interpreted as a coy and calculating silence. "Well—there were only two others. Before you. College boys."

"What about them? Could they make you come?"

Again the cruel silence. Finally she said, "All men are the same."

"I see."

"Most men. Some are different. . .or so I've heard." Pause. "Besides a man doesn't *make* a woman come, as you call it. He works with her."

"I see. He works with her." (Works!) I thought of my last Chinese fortune cookie, the one I got at the Old Peking Restaurant on Speedway after I'd eaten my favorite Chinese dinner, Combination Plate #2. The joker's cookie. "All men are the same," my little slip of paper said, "they only think of one thing. Luckily every woman has one." I thought of the female sexual organ in its outward manifestation. Vulva, inner and outer labia, clitoris, etc.

Never did envy the gynecologist. All those business hours spent peering into that same bearded oyster-like aperture. Not that a man's dangling genital apparatus is half so pretty. A nude woman, if attractive, is a pleasure to look at, but a naked man is merely a man with his pants off—ridiculous.

I thought about these things while Elaine stared wanly into space, and said—but what could I say? I was shocked. Appalled. Devastated. Bored. I said, "I'm sorry, Elaine, good christ. What about jacking off? Can you come that way?"

"Don't be crude. Girls don't—women don't—do that."

"Oh no?"

"Women masturbate."

"And you can come that way?"

"We don't 'come.' We orgasm."

"You what?"

"We orgasm. That's the proper word, in case you don't know."

"Orgasm is not a verb." My anger was stirred again; this really roused me. "Not a verb. Never was, never will be, not once."

"It is now. Orgasming is a verb."

"God's curse on such a verb. You can't do that to our noble American language. You shall not verbalize nouns. I hate that bastard jargon: She 'orgasmed' all over the croutons. Then on the futons. Mr. & Mrs. Turkeyballs 'parented' three kids from birth to the Juvenile Detention Center. The critics 'savaged' his latest masterpiece. You can't do that. I hate it hate it hate it."

"You're going to have to change your ways and attitudes, Henry. Join the modern world. You're twenty years behind the times."

"That's much too close."

Screwing her courage to the sticking point, she stuck it to me. "I hate to say this, Henry, but—you know, you're not a good lover. You're lousy, in fact. You've got to learn some technique."

Ah, technique, technique—another ominous and chilling word. And when they say I hate to say this you know they love it.

Nevertheless: I tried. I was a dutiful husband, in my humble fashion, and I wanted to be a good husband. A good doobie. A modern American hubby. So we worked at it. For an hour that night. And for hours and hours every night afterwards for weeks, for months. Refining the old technique. I worked hard, tinkering with her delicate and complicated genitalia, especially the *Kleitoris* (Gr.), key to a woman's heart. Studied the cliterature. I became intimately familiar with the human cunt—and unlike some I've known, Elaine's was a sweet one. Tasty. The savor, the flavor, the clitoral knob that opens the door, slick as snot on a doorknob. With lips, tongue and fingertips, with toes and nose and eyelashes, I did me best. (Your best is none too good, Lightcap.) I learned to eyeball the labia minora at close range without blinking. And as we know but few will confess, the female sexual organism—and I do mean organism—is not *in itself*, considered apart from context, what you might consider a thing of beauty. A thing of beauty is a joy forever.

We worked hard at sex. And when you have to work at it it's hard work. Every time I pulled off my jeans I felt like I should be punching a time clock.

The Joy of Sex!—Elaine brought home that dreary tract one day, those tidings of comfort and joy by some ex-Commie

Californicated Englishman, and we studied the ghastly pictures, the 365 different positions described. What a joyless book. That poor fucker the instructor-model, performing his gymnastic routines over and over, with slight variations, for 400 pages, each and every time upon *the same woman*. No wonder he has that look on his soft unisex transient's face of a bored he-dog hooked up on the street with an exhausted bitch, longing to leave but unable to extricate himself from what breeders call a "tie." The woman in the book looks no happier; somebody out of mercy should have emptied a bucket of icewater on the miserable couple. Technique, technique, technical engineering, curse of the modern world, debasing what should be a wild, free, lewd, spontaneous act of violent delight into an industrial procedure. Comfort's treatise is a training manual, a workbook which might better have been entitled *The Job of Sex*.

"Christ, Elaine, *Playboy*'s better than this."

"*Playboy* is a sexist magazine."

"I know, it exploits men, $3.00 a copy now. But at least there's a faintly erotic aspect to the pictures. At least there's some dim humor in it. Good cartoons."

"Sex is not a laughing matter."

How true. Yes, she actually said that, I heard it. That's what those dreadful women and those insidious books had done to my good sweet innocent young Elaine. The seduction of ideas. But even she grew weary of some of it.

"We haven't tried this one yet. Number 149."

"I don't want to," she said.

"Why not?"

"It's too humiliating."

"This *book* is humiliating. A sick commercial insult to the human soul." And I flung it—*flang* it!—against the bedroom wall. As I would an obnoxious cat. "To hell with that garbage, Elaine, let's just fuck for the fun of it. No more contortions. No more contractions. No more Hindu-Hebrew-California masochism. Fucking *can* be fun, honey, honest, I remember I clearly remember. Let's throw this Levantine garbage away and make a baby."

That shook her. "A baby? With you?"

"Why not?"

"I'm only 20 years old. I have my career ahead of me." (Which career is that, I wondered.) "I refuse to be forced into woman's traditional role. Would you help?"

"Help what?"

"Change diapers? Bathe it? Feed it?"

"Feed it? You're the one with the tits, how could I feed it? That's your job. Would I feed it, of course not; I'll keep you fed though, that's my job, I'll bring home the pigmeat, keep a roof above our heads in wintertime; I won't change diapers but I'll buy the damn things." Assembly of Japanese bicycle require great peace of mind. What would my friend George Santayana say to this? He said, It takes patience to appreciate domestic bliss. My friend Nietzsche? He said, The married philosopher is a figure out of a stage farce. And Montaigne? He said—but I forget. No I don't. He said, Marriage is like a gilded birdcage: the birds on the outside want in, those on the inside want out. What did they know? Lamely I went on. "You know how an Eskimo woman cleans her baby? up there in the frozen wasteland of the Arctic North?"

"I hate know-it-alls."

"I know it. Do you know?"

"No. And I don't care."

"With her tongue, that's how. In the winter, when there's nothing else available. But that was before ski-planes, snow machines, Prudhoe Bay, welfare and progress. Now they live on Kleenex, Kotex, Pyrex, Tampax, Pampers, Huggies, Oreo Cookies, Holsum Bread and the Federal dole like everyone else, up there in the ice-banana republic of Alaska. An heroic way of life reduced to soap opera in tract-slum ghettos in Fairbanks, Anchorage and Seattle. Did you come this time?"

"You mean did I orgasm? No."

Poor Elaine. I cuddled her close, kissed and caressed her, murmured sweet lies into her ear—and dozed off. Dimly as in a dream I felt her slip from our bed, sobbing, and creep on barefeet into the bathroom. I cried too and fell asleep. I did not hear her return.

All that hard work and nothing gained. Love in the western world. High cuisine and gourmet sex, nothing worked. Disaster loomed above us like the ninth wave at Massacre Beach. Sure, I loved her as much or more than ever but love alone is not enough for anybody. Some fool of a poet said, We must love one another or die. (Auden—that queer, creepy fellow.) But we're going to die anyway—he forgot about that.

No, Elaine needed something more than mere love, whether romantic, matrimonial, conjugal or sexual. She needed something that neither I nor any man, alone and unaided, could give her. What is it? I have my theories. She needed what humans need: a sense of community. Interesting, dignified and essential work to do. (Like finding food or raising a baby.) Connections with the past and future of family, clan, kinfolk, tribe, race. And most of all—I suspect—ownership of a piece of the earth, possession of enough land to guarantee the pride and dignity and freedom that only economic independence can bestow. Without that, what are we? Dependents, that's what. Employees. Personnel. Peasants. Serfs. Slaves. Less than men, less than women. Sub-humans. But this need is so deep and ancient that most people have lost even the consciousness of it. Only the instinct remains. What's the first thing the nouveau-riche do with their money? They buy a big place in the country with barns, pastures, horses, fields. And white fences. And rightly so.

Meantime her feminism hardened, becoming militant and embittered. She not only read but thrust into my hands those awful books, insisting that *I* read them: Greer & Rich & Sarton & Plath & Olsen & Millet & Walker & Brownmiller & Steinem & Co.—a maddened horde of scribbling women. Grudgingly at first, then with deepening incredulity, I read the books. Fascinated, I learned that for the past 50,000 years, or ever since the end of the mythical Golden Age of Matriarchy, human society has been operated solely and exclusively for the benefit of men, that we men have conspired together for numberless generations to persecute, oppress, repress and enslave our own wives, mothers, grandmothers, sisters, daughters, grand-daughters, nieces, sweethearts, lovers, mistresses, and female friends.

A fascinating and fantastical tale. An intellectual neurosis for which our psychiatric technicians have yet to devise a name. But as always, the more preposterous the doctrine the more fanatic its adherents. There is no animal so spooky as the true believer. We argued, in and out of bed, for hours, days, weeks:

Certainly, I agreed, males dominate females. In every known human (and mammalian) society this is and has been the case. The explanation is so simple and obvious it escapes the observation of feminist intellectuals: men are bigger, stronger, more aggressive. Intelligence, morality, justice have little to do with it. The rule of law means the rule of those who make the law, interpret it, enforce it. Bulk counts. Might does not make right but it makes what is. As Georg Wilhelm Friedrich Hegel pointed out, in his 26-volume footnote to Plato, "Vat effer iss, iss right."

"But," Elaine said—

I ranted on: Women the victims, men the victors? Tell it to the Marines. Tell it to those grunts, all boys, who sweated, fought, suffered and died in the green hell of Vietnam while their majors and colonels circled above them in helicopters, observing, chewing cigars, barking insane irrational incomprehensible commands. Tell it to the serfs of merrie England who plowed, sowed, reaped and saw the fruits of their labor stolen from them by the lords— and ladies—who claimed ownership of the land. A claim enforced by sword lance club mace the noose the rack the wheel the fire. Tell it to Faulkner and the slaves of the Deep South ("God shat upon the earth and He called it—Mississippi"). Tell it to the indentured bondsmen and girls (Tillie Ostrander) of Old Virginia. Tell it to Big Bill Haywood, Joe Hill, Wesley Everest and the ghosts of the IWW. Tell it to Emma Goldman, Mother Jones, Elizabeth Gurley Flynn and Rosa Luxembourg. Tell it to Jack Cade, Wat Tyler, Ned Ludd, Nat Turner, John Brown. Tell it to Diogenes

and H. Thoreau. Tell it to those who died in the Coliseum, to
Spartacus and the 20,000 slaves, all men, who were crucified with
him by the victorious Romans. Tell it to the slaves—men, women,
children—who built the Pyramids, the Great Wall of China, the
Parthenon, the Appian viaducts, the walls of Toledo and Burgos,
the Taj Mahal, the city of Macchu Pichu, the cannibal temples of
Mexico, the lost and forgotten horrors of imperial Africa. Tell it to
the people who pick our bananas, our coffee beans, our tea leaves,
our tomatoes strawberries grapes and lettuce. Tell it to Aleksandr
I. Sohlzenitsyn and the surviving *zeks* of the Gulag and the KGB.
Tell it to Lech Walesa. Tell it to the ghosts of Eugene Debs,
Norman Thomas, John L. Lewis. Tell it to the coal miners, the
steel puddlers, the chemical workers, the uranium miners, the
school teachers. Tell it to Jean Valjean. Tell it to Leo Tolstoy, Peter
Kropotkin, Michael Bakunin, Nestor Mahkno, Taras Bulba, Errico
Malatesta, Ramón Sender, Pablo Barruti, Pancho Villa, Emiliano
Zapata and B. Traven.

"But," Elaine began again—

Yes, I agreed, most women have been victims, right alongside
their husbands, sons and brothers, ever since the invention of
plantation agriculture and the urban conglomeration (two dreadful
setbacks for equality, liberty, democracy and humanity). Most
women, like their men, have been peons and cottonpickers,
factory hands and office clerks, service workers and wage slaves—
subjects. Yes. But—

"But," Elaine insisted—

—but, I agreed, not *all* women, not quite *all* men. For the
women of the rich and powerful, life is and always has been

different. Do you think the lady of the manor would change places with a male field hand? Would England's Princess Diana give up her soft role for the part of a dock worker tramping home to his kennel in the slums? Huh? The great division in the social pyramid is not between the sexes but between the classes. The gulf is horizontal not vertical. 60% of the wealth of the U.S.A. belongs to 2% of American families. When the manly galley slaves of imperial Egypt toiled so desperately at the oars of the great trireme, who was that long-haired dark and comely personage being towed behind on water skiis? Antony? No ma'am. It was Cleopatra! When Adam delved and Eve span, who was then the gentleman?

"Adam?" she suggested.

"Shut up!" I explained.

"But what I'm trying to tell you—"

"Please. Let me finish." The debate dragged on for another hour, another month, then collapsed without warning when she abruptly gave up feminism for aerobic dancing. Every evening. Feminism was bad for her figure. First things first. Me, neglected husband, I retreated into sexual asceticism. For a week. Then resumed slipping around on the sly, sneaky as a tomcat, subtle as a rooster.

Leading to further controversy. She screamed, I shouted, she quoted, I sneered, she cried I bellowed she slammed the door. Our house crumbled. I won the argument, I think, but lost my wife.

And I never could make her come. Instead of coming she went.

VII

He eats his eggs and sausage, drinks his coffee, gnaws his crust of bread. April sunlight, bright, cruel, heartbreaking, pours into the kitchen through the morning window. The music of McKinley Morgenfield, better known as Muddy Waters, pours from the stereophonic speakers. Good man, old Waters.

Henry eats his breakfast, bleak and lonely, and makes his plans. Plug in phone, call Welfare office, tell them he's taking another leave without pay, they won't mind. Visit bank, empty checking account, pick up needed cash. Load up the old Dodge truck with camping gear, essential firearms, spare parts, a certain few books. Write a farewell letter to Elaine. Shoot the dog. Get in truck and point its battered nose eastward, toward the world of the rising sun and Stump Creek, West Virginia. Home.

Only three thousand five hundred miles to go. Brother Will, I say to my shattered heart, my private little secret, here I come.

Prepare thyself.

JACK CURTIS

Red Knife Valley

VOLUME VII

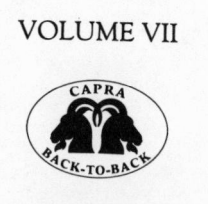

CAPRA PRESS
1986

Cover design by Francine Rudesill
Designed and typeset in Garamond by Jim Cook
SANTA BARBARA, CALIFORNIA

LIBRARY OF CONGRESS CATALOGING-IN-PUBLICATION DATA
Abbey, Edward, 1927-
CONFESSIONS OF HENRY LIGHTCAP, BARBARIAN.
(Capra back-to-back series)
No collective t.p. Titles transcribed from individual title pages.
I. Curtis, Jack, 1922-   .   Red Knife Valley. 1986
II. Title.   III. Title: Red Knife Valley.
PS3551.B2C6   1986   813'.54   85-26939
ISBN 0-88496-244-X (pbk.)

PUBLISHED BY
CAPRA PRESS
Post Office Box 2068
Santa Barbara, Ca. 93120

CONTENTS

ME AND RED KNIFE

I MIND MY OWN business and I don't bother people if they
leave me alone. Muggers sometimes think I'm an easy mark,
and it's a waste because Red Knife won't eat human kind.

Someday I'll find a mate. She is not in the park now, but the call
of the wild will bring her, I know, and we will stick together like a
pair of timber wolves for as long as we live.

I was born on the fourteenth floor of the City Hospital
downtown sixteen years ago. I started reading about nature in the
Carnegie Library when I was about eight, that makes eight years
I've studied pioneers and Indians and living off the land.

I wanted to be an Indian, an Iroquois, master of snares and
feathered lances, bows and flint headed arrows. But by the time I
was nine, I knew those days were long gone.

Mother was fat and worked a Singer sewing machine. She
wouldn't encourage me to learn about nature so I did it the hard
way. I discovered my secret friend, Red Knife.

When I was ten I built a trap on the fire escape. I made it out of an old lace curtain and two coat hangers, and I caught a male White Throated Sparrow. This sparrow is distinguished by a bright yellow patch between beak and eye.

After I examined my catch, I realized there was no cage to put it in. I let Red Knife decide whether to free the bright-eyed beating bird or kill it. Red Knife counted coup and hacked his head off and worked an hour to pick off the feathers and disembowel the prey. Red Knife roasted him over the gas burner and ate him. He was tough but nourishing and tasted gamey.

We ate a lot of sparrows that winter. Vesper Sparrows, an Evening Grosbeak, even an Indigo Bunting that had missed its migration south.

I learned about survival of the fittest.

Mother begrudged my zeal. She wouldn't help dress the birds or eat them either. We went our separate ways even though we lived in the same room.

That spring in a secluded meadow in the park I made a simple wire snare which I placed in a travel worn animal path that meandered through the weeds.

Next morning I found the stiffened brown body of an Eastern Cottontail. He had hung himself on Red Knife's noose. As I was examining its powderpuff tail, a gardener came rushing up, yelling and disturbing the quiet natural primitiveness of the meadow. When I said that Red Knife caught the rabbit, he shook my shoulder and took away Red Knife's rabbit and threw it in a ditch. Then he marched me to an office where I got a lecture on how to conduct myself in a public park. Then, like they were

doing me a big favor, they let me loose. It was like mother always saying, "Go forth and sin no more."

I didn't go back to the park for the rest of the summer. Instead, I caught lots of birds and I invented a teeter-totter trap that tipped greedy mice into a coffee can half full of water. Red Knife wouldn't eat the mice, saying they should be used as bait to catch bigger prey.

Brown Norwegian Rats invaded our building in the fall and I discovered a worthy adversary.

Using a plastic bucket in place of a coffee can, I improved on my teeter-totter mouse trap and had good success, but its rat capacity was limited. I had no luck with snare or deadfall.

Red Knife grew tired of eating fried or roasted rats, so I went to a sports shop, draped a rubber slingshot around my neck and under my shirt and walked out. I used wheel balance weights pried off of parked cars for ammunition, and in a few weeks I could shoot as good as Davy Crockett. I could hit a snowbird at fifty paces.

I told a girl Red Knife ate rats and she told everybody in school.

In my studies I learned about natural herbs the pioneers and Indians used for cooking their game. A large collection of herbs flourished in the Botanical Gardens and they were left unattended during the lunch hour. My sharp butcher knife and a brown paper bag were all that was needed to provide me with sage, rosemary and sweet basil, and many others.

Several nourishing, tasty vegetables and greens grew in the Parkway divider which I could identify and harvest after I'd

dodged through the traffic. Once a cabbie nearly ran over me and he yelled, "Hey stupid, you crazy!"

My mother grew fatter on TV dinners and canned mushroom soup, but Red Knife ate natural foods which he reaped from the wilderness and he grew stronger and more clever. His eye saw clearly, his mind was always busy solving the problems of natural life.

Leaning idly against a maple tree, covertly watching for gardeners or those people who go into the shrubbery, I waited until the coast was clear. Whipping out the slingshot loaded with a one ounce lead weight, Red Knife quick aimed and hit a red squirrel in the head, dropping him stone cold dead instantly. The whole procedure took no more time than it takes to breathe deeply once.

Strolling along with my brown paper bag, I settled down by my squirrel, slipped him into the bag, and departed for my feast.

Domestic pigeons or Rock Dove were too easy for fun, but a plump pigeon breast roasted with sweet butter and fresh thyme is a rare treat and I became adept at selecting my birds for tenderness. You can tell by the redness of the band between the bill and head. "The redder the better," Livereater Jackson, the mountainman, said.

Catching pigeons was simple. On the roof of the building I leaned a square of wire mesh above the tar and gravel. Then scattering bread or Quaker Oats under it, I would wait behind the chimney until the pigeons landed and started to feed. In a few minutes they would be under the mesh, and when I would come out they would try to fly upward, get their beaks through the

mesh, and since they don't know how to fly backwards, there was always a lot of shiny blue heads and red beaks poking through the mesh. Red Knife picked out the ones with the reddest beaks and cut their heads off with the butcher knife, and released the rest.

They never learned.

I quit school because I had read most of the pioneering and Indian books and the books on outdoor lore, so there was no point wasting my time on Geometry and such courses.

This gave me more time for nature experiments and more time to practice. I was five foot eleven, weighed one hundred sixty pounds, and I wore moccasins.

Mother never even noticed I wasn't going to school anymore. She was fat as a pig from watching TV. I never cost her a penny because I ate only fresh killed game and fresh picked greens.

Exploring the south end of the park, I found fish ponds and marshland. When I saw the giant goldfish fanning slowly through the water, I felt a new and eager hunger.

Red Knife could have laughed and simply speared the fish, but the patrolling hostile guards made my stalk more difficult and exciting.

I already had some string and I went downtown and stole a fish hook. I noticed the goldfish ate a lot of bread that people tossed into the pond, so I baited my hook with a wad of old bread. Then I pulled the string up through the right leg of my overalls and stood close to the bank with my baited hook on down in the water.

A big orange goldfish with a fan tail lazily found my bait and sucked it down. Quickly I jerked on my string and had him up my pant's leg in half a second.

As I walked away, he flopped ferociously and made a great commotion until I got into the shrubbery where Red Knife counted coup and killed him.

He wasn't as succulent as I'd hoped. Later when I discovered the Rainbow Trout pond with its pretty splashing fountain, I used the same procedure with great success, catching four pound trout easily any day except weekends when there were too many on-lookers.

I learned many ways of preparing the big trout from cookbooks in the Carnegie Library. They are easy unless you get into Trout Puffs or Truite Bleu.

Ducks and geese swam on the pond, doing nothing. They were tame from having been there several generations and from people throwing bread and popcorn at them.

I'd never tasted duck before, and I started counting guards and groundskeepers. Most of the sport of the hunt is in the preparation.

As usual the solution was simple, but it needed some stage dressing. I snagged a little radio and carried a blanket and a book to the far side of the pond, took my shirt off and lay down to read about Kit Carson. I did that for several days until the guards weren't even seeing me anymore. When I figured they believed me to be just another stupid kid, I brought my string and fish hook and baited it with a wad of bread.

The first duck I ever caught was a male Pintail with a lovely shiny green head. Red Knife whipped him out of the water and smothered him under my blanket so fast he never knew what hit him. Nobody else did either. I found the duck superb, especially when roasted with chutney and orange slices.

Teal, Widgeons, Blacks all went for my hook that summer and I lived like a king of the wilderness. Later on in the fall I went for the Canadian Geese and Brant.

My mother kept giving me dirty looks, and when I'd offer to share my gourmet dinner, she would huff and puff and call me names like I was some kind of an animal.

She kept saying I should get a job like everybody else.

By then I was strong as a pioneer, brown as an Indian, wore my hair in two braids, and no one knew what I knew.

I felt strong enough to try for a bear.

The bears were kept on a big concrete island surrounded by a moat of water and a chainlink fence. They had plenty of guards loafing around too.

Every time I looked at the bears, my mouth would fill up with spit, and Red Knife would say, "Kill me a bear."

When it snowed, the bears hibernated in concrete caves. The moat around the island froze solid. I made a crossbow out of a car spring and my arrows were short lengths of steel reinforcing bars. Like Daniel Boone I was loaded for bear.

Christmas Eve when the guards were drunk and the bears were asleep, I went hunting.

Red Knife found a prime brown bear with the flashlight and shot him through the head with the re-bar and he made not a sound when he died.

Red Knife counted coup, dragged him out of the cave and skinned him with the butcher knife. He took the loin back-straps, and then he covered up the carcass with snow, climbed back over the fence, and went home for a jolly Christmas dinner.

The pelt took more time to tan that I expected, but I worked it out with ashes and fat until it made a good blanket for my bed in the corner of the kitchen.

My mother was so fat she couldn't bend over to tie her shoes. She wore floppy felt slippers and shuffled around flippity-floppity like a Snowshoe Rabbit.

They were tearing down the old buildings. Every week another tenement in the block went crashing into a pile of moldy bricks. Mother said we had to move. She kept nagging that I would have to get a job.

I said I didn't need a job. I was sixteen years old and I had no need for money, but she kept saying I had to earn money to keep a roof over our heads, and I said I don't need a roof, I don't need anything except the butcher knife and my bearskin, and she kept saying what about me and then one day she looked at me out of the corner of her eye, and I knew she was not only a useless burden to me, she was also dangerous. Red Knife would end up in an asylum.

Red Knife shot her through the head with a re-bar.

I filled my backpack with crossbow, fish hook, snare wire, wire mesh, dutch oven, butcher knife, and bearskin, and moved into the park.

Just at daybreak, when a veil of eastern light comes across the glow of the city, the park seems to change into a new beautiful country. A peacock screams, the wolf howls one last time, and lions roar and grumble. The big trees straighten up and dew floats on the lawns, and the flowers all over begin to open up and make the morning smell so sweet and pure, I always wonder why there is no one awake, no one aware of the dawn.

SYCAMORE

OUT OF THE MAYPOLE striped soul where origins twine, from the luminous seethings of moonmist under shadowed trees she became herself; first a single-toothed serpent rapacious for any uterine aureole, ripping the membrane to be swallowed in turn, digested, synthesized, and as soon as she could, she called herself Sycamore.

Her parents named her Gloria after a rich aunt, a second-hand label on sale, but Sycamore knew she was a tree. Before she could talk, she knew pine and mulberry, chestnut and maple, but she saw herself twinned to the silver-barked Sycamore—Praise be to God for dappled things—carrying great meandering limbs twigged with velvety green stars.

For several years, the Shepherds proudly believed they were blessed with a gifted child, mensa-minded at least, because of her eloquent gestures, her immediate knowing of the usual disciplines, her independence.

15

But when it became certain that she was a genius, able to absorb any vocabulary and dispense from it in multisyllabic, explicit phrases, having voraciously mastered the three R's and phased out paperdolls and coloring books, she took upon herself a habit of silence, standing by as a small watchperson or witness, responding, if at all, with a yes or no, and seeding the cloud of loving euphoria that hovered over her parents' dimensional minds with bitter crystals of doubt and guilt.

"What have we done?" they asked the How-To books, and were advised in tarpits of verbiage that she needed more love, patience, and understanding. "What have you done?" they asked each other suspiciously and, without patience or understanding, blamed the other for injecting neurosis into the once radiantly strong child.

Sycamore could have told them she felt fine, but speech had become an obnoxious intrusion of her serenity as well as a waste of time, since most of it was false.

Mr. Shepherd, tall and stooped, a quiet man who would rather have been a banker than a real-estate broker, paced the floor like a heron seeking young trout in the nylon carpet.

His wife, Maxine, the flibberty-gibbet of the pair, trotted from the kitchen haven to living room, straightening the glossy magazines on the coffee table, blitzing a phrase, retreating to the kitchen, and back again.

"Don't blame me!"

"I'm not blaming," he replied, slowly circling the glass-topped table. "I'm trying to explain that Gloria's tests are very expensive."

On her return, Maxine smoothed the print cover of a wingchair,

and snapped off another quick shot, "You should have thought of that. . . ."

"When?" he asked as she hurried back into the kitchen. "What could I have done?"

"You could have held her more. Cuddled. Bonded!"

"Possibly," he nodded vigorously, "possibly, but someone has to earn the wherewithal. These tests. . . ."

"An institution costs a lot more!" she cried over her shoulder.

His shoulders hunched a notch more, and his hopes for a simple, conclusive balance faded. Day by day they would go, one step at a time, into time, into farewell: a futile fade away into the darkness ahead.

And the girl upstairs, what would happen to her? Would electric shock bring her back? Ritalin, Lithium, hormones, aspirin? You could tell her a tree was a tree and a person a person, you could hire an expensive therapist to say the same thing, but not a whit of it got through.

"She'll grow out of it," his mother had advised.

"Too bad," his Aunt Gloria spoke with the finality of an undertaker.

"It's just a stunt to get attention, pay her no mind," Maxine's mother had laughed.

"Who knows? Maybe she'll turn out to be a brilliant tree surgeon," Harry, his brother-in-law, had guffawed. Maxine's family never took things seriously.

None of them seemed to feel the urgency and the gravity of the problem. Of course she wasn't completely autistic, and she didn't torture kittens, and she was harmless and docile, but why

was she always climbing trees? Why did she sew leaves together
and make jungle costumes? Why did she pull back in the fall and
grow nearly dormant in winter, becoming a bloodless, great-eyed
ghost, saved only by the coming of spring and robust summer?

They couldn't send her to school in the winter, she lacked the
energy. And when they did force her to go, the school nurse would
send her home with a nasty note.

And of course the neighbors pretended sympathy and pretended anxiety, pretended anything to get an emotional chop from the
family abattoir.

And what would happen this spring? She was growing,
developing, a swelling bud, and the world outside was a cruel and
heartless battlefield, filthy and vicious.

"Sooner or later," he said, pacing the words to his judgemental
stride, "she must be placed in an institution for special care and
protection."

"Are you saying I'm not looking after her well enough?"
Maxine cried from the kitchen. "Are you accusing me?"

"Please, he said, vexed with her obstinance, "there is no guilt or
blame."

It was time-wasting to carry on a discussion that had never
really come to the discussing stage, never had, never would.

Better to be dealing, finding capital, locating properties, developing. How could he talk Nicholas Lyme into subdividing his
acreage next door? Call it Lyme Manors. A development like that,
complete with shopping center, would set them up for the rest of
their lives.

He could faintly hear Gloria humming in her room, a strange,

off-key, wordless song that reminded him of music he'd heard somewhere as a child, a harmless idle threnody which, when he heard it in his own home, his heart sank in abject defeat.

Maxine darted from the kitchen grotto to the stairwell and shrieked, "Gloria, stop that noise!"

Sycamore heard the strident command and took a deep breath to stop her long, humming song. She had no desire to annoy anyone, especially her parents. She had no particular goal in life, no urge to reform ghetto children or to bring prosperity to Peruvians, no talent for art, no desire to love a Movie Star and start a family, and what intellectual quickness had once been foremost in her mind, was now vitiated in the whole sky, day and night.

The sky of her mind formed the sky of tall pine trees. Sun, moon, and stars in that sky belonged to the steadfast arboreal realm in which she lived.

That sky was most beautiful once you had the vision of it, most tranquil, most demanding in storms, often critical in backbreaking gusts, but the power of that transcendence was so infinite and lovely, she knew of nothing anywhere close to comparable value.

And she saw herself in the mirror, tall and brown, budding breasts, a lean-boned form filling to soft and curious shapes like dollops of ice cream, and her short-cut hair silver, almost transparent as young sycamore leaves. Her face made a simple composition of pale green eyes, straight down nose, straight across mouth. Mainly it was the soft, fine silver hair she saw, the rest was meaningless. Each leaf is suited to its own bird, she thought.

Limbs, crotches and nests, and leaves like snowflakes in their infinite designs, not geometrical but liquid, etheric. Does that make water crystalline and fiber fluid? And why then did they call her crazy when no one had tried to consider the world from the center of a maple tree?

In the afternoon she'd taken off her clothes and climbed through the big maple, testing branches with her weight. Hearing a protest, she'd moved back to stronger boughs, apologizing, "There now, it's all right."

It was most pleasing to work gently and patiently up through the center of the great tree, through the leafy light all pale green and shimmering until her head popped out into the direct sunshine like a chick poking its head from under a hen's wing. To gain the sun, to stand on the fluid masthead tree, to flow over the fluid green sea in the crow's nest. "Land Ho! Sou Sou West by Sou West, mate!"

To imagine sailing west across the continent of grass, across the purple green conifer forests, seeking the lost continent of the Pacific!

And after that, after sighting the cape of sun in the pure verdance, no private school, no blue wool skirt and white blouse could teach her differently. No humor, no rightness, no style, nor comraderie could uncape the sun nor undress the green of her body.

And after that, no counselor's wry whimsy or wanton eye, no buck-up hand on the shoulder, or exact two fingers on the knee, no slow-paced spoken sisterhood, no couch, or inkblot, could come between Sycamore and her sailing the tree of life.

After that, after that swaying mastery of earth and heaven from her wren's perch, no pill, upper or downer, no infusion of camomile, no injection of ascorbate, no sulfur and molasses, no anode or diode, no hot bath or cold shower, no basket weaving, pottery making, leather work or stitchery could dilute the tree-being, the nymph and druid of the forest, nor quiet the breeze in the boughs, nor frighten the birds from their secure nests. No man-made lightning could split her trunk nor any chemical herbicide wither her identity.

She had to outgrow it, the interested bystanders advised. As she grew she would be too heavy, too clumsy, for the skyward choreography of a nymph.

And in a way, it was true.

As a little girl, her friendship with the birds in the trees had been cute, but now it seemed grotesque. No longer the picture of innocence, Sycamore was seen by friends and neighbors as a warped weirdo. They didn't call her that. They called her 'poor thing,' 'unfortunate,' 'mentally retarded,' 'educationally deprived.' Now the taunts of her peers were sharper and meaner. Once they'd chased her, teasing, through the branches, but now they stayed rooted in the dirt, and with loud shouts and cries, threw their muddy wonder, "Loony bird!" "Tree witch!" "Squirrely-ass!"

She remained silent as forest floor, disappearing behind a tree trunk, moving farther within the ranks where great trees would dampen the tormentors' cries, soak them up like humous until she could hear nothing except the breeze harp and the feel of birds.

Her parents were helpless. Money spent and nothing to show for it. Their imagination had been extended as far as it could

stretch and it still could not climb from earth to sky, and in desperation they threw in with their neighbors and friends, attending parties and discussing what the media had already pre-digested, working for the wage and seeking out the bargains, starting up a little money-fund account and getting back to normal.

Sycamore appreciated their forbearance. She could come and go through the unlocked back door, could sleep when she was tired and study any world she liked. She appreciated the leftovers in the refrigerator and she left her room and the bathroom immaculate as if she'd never been there.

She learned to trim her lengthening silver hair into a sleek helmet, secure from bothersome brush and occasional barbs and thorns.

People said, "Don't worry, she'll grow out of it." But her parents despaired as the years went by and nothing seemed to help, nothing changed for the better.

And now Sycamore was coming to the time her parents feared and hoped for, when the chemistry of maturity shoots new compounds into dormant glands and the whole world turns into an often unbearable reality.

Nothing happened. Her mother fretted and nosed about through the laundry and the bathroom and found not a clue. Pointless to have a heart-to-heart, woman-to-woman discussion. You might as well talk sex to a cabbage.

Even so, her mother bought pertinent books and left them in conspicuous places, thankful that if there was no riddle, there was no need of solution.

The trees burgeoned with fragile mouse-ear leaves and the sap was pumping up from the roots, but Sycamore hardly changed except to grow a little taller.

Briarcliff merchants brought out their seeds and lawnmowers and plastic water hoses for sale, and her mother felt an awful dread in the pit of her stomach that every year was going to be the same stasis, a cold misery of continuum, nothing changing for better, for worse, no older or wiser. . . . How long, how long, O Lord?

Definitely Sycamore was growing into a young adult, filling out, coming into her growth, and by the time she was sixteen they were terrified that she still might develop into womanhood.

She didn't worry about it. Her friends lived outside with roots in the ground and their heads in the sky. That was most important. What she didn't know about sex meant to her no more than what she didn't know about death.

They harbored thoughts of an operation, dark, unadmitted thoughts never spoken, but the finality of sterility was too much to try. Suppose the light suddenly dawned in her mind that she was human, a human woman? Suppose then she wanted children, and all she had was a scar pleating her flat, hard tummy? She might just revert back into arboreal splendor.

And what would happen to her when they were old and pensioned off? Who would care for her when they passed on?

If only she'd do something bad! Kill birds or drown dogs, run nude down the street, scream shocking things out the upstairs window, make her bodily functions out in the open, write threats to the Mayor or the Minister.

Some of Briarcliff's citizens felt a sense of empathy with the girl, admitting with a smile that they wished they too could find something somewhere in this mortal world as clean and true as a tree to love.

But there were others, whose ideas of innocence and freedom were warped by self-inflicted shabbiness, who would have Sycamore sent away before she 'did' something. Those minds would have been more comfortable and avenged if she'd been legally killed.

Yet in time, as often happens, the community encapsulated her within its own body like an integument grown around an irremoveable sliver, rendering it painless and without danger.

The hardware dealers no longer worried that she might attack their displays of axes and chain saws. The newspaper no longer concerned itself with the possibility she might resent its waste of paper. Homebuilders and lumber dealers no longer felt hostile to her freedom because she traveled her own road.

For Sycamore, the best walking was in the Nicholas Lyme estate next door to her own home. The Lyme mansion, separated by a low stone wall and buffered by sixty acres of wilderness was easy to avoid, and Mr. Lyme lived by himself and hardly even bothered about the grounds.

Tall she strolled in the woodlands, her silver hair lifting in the lightest breeze, her large green eyes roving, her slender arms loose and easy, her supple fingers caressing the trunks of old friends as she followed any winding path into dappled shadows and sunlight.

Sometimes, like a fat house cat eye-balling a pigeon on a gravel

path, Mr. Lyme did stray occasionally into his woodlands, catching sight of the slender girl as she roved over her own familiar paths.

Certainly Mr. Lyme had as much right as she to walk the land if only because he held the deed to the estate and all chattel thereon. Others in the community could have invaded the wild estate, but hunting was better north of town, birdwatching and camping better to the west near the lake. This forest was too tangled with wild grape and bittersweet vines to make leisure walking a pleasure. Oddly, yes, she herself walked alone there with pleasure because she knew her own secret webbed paths, and no one else tried them and not even Mr. Lyme walked with pleasure through the woods.

Yet he appeared here and there, no more than that. Not hounding, not sniffing out the spoor, not lying in wait, just appearing at odd times. His leather-pipped tweed coat buttoned and belted neatly around his cock robin's form, his twiggy legs clad in worsted wool, carrying a brass ferruled walking stave with an ivory lion's head, an Irish cap on his large bald and freckled skull, a creature pelted from long dead and distant sheep, an alien dandy in the reality of copses of beeches and beds of ferns.

She usually sensed him before she saw him poking along her fragile ways, and she would silently disappear, either leaving for the day or moving into the most tangled, swampy areas where she could climb above the tangle and swing through the tops of the tall trees while he poked along in a friendlier corner of the estate.

In time, of course, he tried to talk to her, tried to catch her attention, sometimes calling, 'Hello, girl, hello, girl, don't be afraid.'.

But she recognized in him an alien kind of creature, different from the denizens of the woods or the shopkeepers on Market Street. She felt no resentment for the vipers that inhabited her world, nor for the occasional child who hooted at her, but this unusual person belonged outside her world and she would no more converse with him than she would cuddle an axe.

Sometimes he would shout at the trees where he thought she'd hidden, "Come out, girl, nothing to fear here.", but Sycamore didn't respond. She was long gone. She had no need for both of them in the forest.

But he resented her aloofness. Why shouldn't she at least say hello to him? She didn't have to curtsy or drag a leg or claw a forelock, all she had to do was politely say, 'Goodmorning, sir.'. Why couldn't she respond just that much?

He persisted, but her instincts were always miles ahead of him, and he found himself as frustrated as a man trying to catch smoke in his hand.

It was not in his nature to accept defeat, to co-exist with an enigma.

And now he bounded along like an enraged jaybird, over the tiny trails, driving instead of dancing from one bare spot to the next. His own exertions stamped out defined avenues in the forest, bruised and trampled by his own weight, and it was a combination of these regular passages and his anger at being ignored that set him along a more dangerous course.

After two weeks of stalking, searching, hiding in blinds, and heavy pursuit, he finally caught a glimpse of her in profile, slender as an otter and dancing with a deer's grace off into the thickets,

and he stopped and pounded his stave on the white, soft trunk of a birch and shouted after her, "I'll get a bulldozer! By God, I'll get a bulldozer and show you a thing or two!"

Next day he made it so. The yellow iron Caterpillar with its ripping, polished blade followed him as he guided the way through the woods, making avenues wide enough for a truck, ripping up the humous where rings of mushrooms had grown forever, yanking out the birches by their roots and slamming them into piles of trash beside the trails, flattening the once cool ferns.

On that day Sycamore left the woods and returned to her nest in the great maple in her backyard and lay with a fever.

In the night she returned to the park, quietly weeping as she walked the new and sap bleeding roads, the bare dirt without a touch of life or spring to it, the trashed trees dying in an agony that made the night infamous in its carnage as Austerlitz or Hiroshima.

She stubbed her toes and scabbed her feet on broken rocks that had always been buried beneath a carpet of humous.

And she felt a heavy remorse, a guilt she'd never known before. If she had only accepted the creature bobbing along and shouting, perhaps this disaster might not have happened. She knew as well as she knew green leaves that the massacre of her beloved wilderness was her own fault.

Next day Sycamore waited for him near the raw scarification. She knew he was coming long before she heard him. He was alone.

She waited in her concealment as he bounded along. She had taken a bittersweet vine from the trash by the road, a vine that

had once reached the sun, sap upward from the root pressed, at
the top of a maple tree, but both maple and vine lay ripped and
uprooted alongside the new road. Fibers, limp dirty leaves, torn
and crushed, and no more the sap to travel in beauty from bog to
sun up the vine that leaned upon the maple boughs for help.

She tried to comfort the tree and the vine in her frightened
hands as Mr. Lyme came bounding in rage and victory up his
rocky road.

Stopping, he addressed the remaining forest as if he knew she
were concealed there, "See there, girl, now you see whose land it
is, now you see I can do what I want with it. I can. Understand,
girl? I can pave it with concrete if I like! And by God, I will too, if
you give me any more of your sauce!"

Sycamore surprised him by quietly stepping out before his eyes
like a tame egret. He stood stunned to silence, eyeing the length of
fresh killed vine in her hands, and said, "I knew you'd come out."

"It was so true," she said. "Why did you kill it?"

He glared at her and stepped forward. She didn't move.

"I just wanted to see you," he said gently. "Is that so bad?"

His eyes were moist as he looked into her own wide green and
silver gaze. His voice trembled and lost its imperative.

"I just want what's mine," he murmured. "Nothing wrong in
that. You're welcome here."

She didn't answer or move in any way, neither repellant or
seductive, but he couldn't abide hiatus. He was a mover and a
shaker. He believed that if you're not moving, you're fooling
around.

To break the impasse of silence and immobility, he gambled

and put his hand on her waist. When she didn't move, he put his other hand farther down and paused, smiling at the imaginary victory, and tried to draw her close.

Mr. Lyme was found by his handyman. There were no footprints, fingerprints, or bloodshed. The Westchester County Coroner surmised that poor Mr. Lyme had gotten himself tangled in a bittersweet vine, panicked no doubt, and grabbed at a maple branch to clear himself, only to lose the grip and catch his neck in a limber crotch, just strong enough to keep his feet from touching the earth.

The girl who called herself Sycamore was not missed for several months, not at least until snow fell and then when she didn't return to her upstairs room, Mr. and Mrs. Shepherd reported it to the proper authorities, supplying an old photo, and in that way the silent girl slowly blended into the conforming trees and was gone.

THE CAVE

I FOUND THE CAVE on the other side of the park, away from the avenue. Me and Red Knife scouted the cave, watching the grown over cliffside for several days until we were sure no one used it anymore.

I climbed by a faded No Trespassing sign and entered the cave ready for trouble. I've learned to beware of my own kind, but none of them had used the cave for a long time. The sunlight was mostly absorbed by soot caked on the walls, a product of past years of campfires right here in the middle of the city.

Outside the leaves were already red and falling. There was no turning back. I would not live like a rat in a tenement ever again.

Taking a shovel from a gardener's cart, I went to work cleaning out my cave. All day I dug through layered generations of human filth, heaving cans and bottles out and over the cliff. Winter would hide it all.

I uncovered a bed of moldy newspapers dating back a hundred

30

years and chucked the whole stinking mess over the side. I found an inscription scratched into the limestone wall: God help me and Ireland. P. Sullivan 1867.

Who knows? P. Sullivan could have been my great grandfather.

When the cave was clean enough for a wild animal I brought in my iron pot and my bearskin, my crossbow made of a car spring and the rebar rods I use for arrows, my food cache, knife and axe, and settled in for the winter.

The tenement I left when Red Knife took care of my mother wasn't near as roomy and safe as the cave. In the tenement there was no natural balance. It was a swarm of rats and a swarm of cockroaches all trying to live off a swarm of terrorized people.

Here in the park there are enough cats to catch the rats, and enough birds to match the bugs.

It might be harder to find small game when it snowed. The ducks and geese would be gone, the fish would be below the ice, but I wasn't too worried. There is plenty of big game in the zoo.

I could find corn in the zoo's feedroom and there were plenty of butternuts and black walnuts and chestnuts to be gathered in the grounds below my cave.

I spent a few days storing dead wood inside. I had to work early in the mornings before the groundkeepers came to work, but daybreak is the best time for a self-sufficient hunting man, and my whole system is naturally tuned with the sun.

Outside, on the crowded streets of the city, the people run on mechanical clock time. They run to work in the morning and run back to their shelters eight hours later, and predators of their own kind, lurking in the streets and the halls, pick off the old and the

weak and the stupid, the same as hyenas pick off the wildebeests in Africa.

Often as I roamed the park exploring the far reaches and learning my own habitat, I found pools of human blood, and when I found bodies, I went the other way.

The regular gangs that rob like hyenas leave me alone; maybe because of my size, maybe because I carry the big knife, maybe because of the way I walk. Somehow they know I will explode with my weapon and Red Knife will count coup many times if they ever try to cut me down.

I recognize them. I see their leaders rise up and disappear, and they know I don't care one way or another. They know our world is kill or die, but the difference is that I don't prey on humans. My Indian brother, Red Knife, knows the difference. When he kills, he kills because of a threat against us or for food. That is our code, the same as Jim Bridger or Livereater Johnson.

After Red Knife took care of my flipperty floppity mother who was going to lock us up, he said my new name was Kit, after Kit Carson.

There was a big man, I think he was Russian, whatever he was, he was big. Maybe ten years ago he had been six feet six, but now time and bad food were collapsing him. His muscles were slipping apart and he walked bent over like a baboon and he let his head sway back and forth loosely like a bear when he walked.

Something terrible had happened to him back in the time of his life. He had not always been a shambling giant with a concertina and a monkey on a string.

His mouth sometimes hung open and threads of spit drooled

away like spiderwebs, because he talked to himself a lot. He talked in his own language, and his eyes would roll around anxiously, like he was trying to get a message across: that the ship had sprung a leak, or that the Empire State building was on fire.

The monkey didn't care. He would sway back and forth, dancing to the music the big man squeezed from the concertina. The big man swayed too and they made a funny pair dancing to the music.

When the song was finished, the monkey would pick up the nickels and dimes the tourists tossed out, but sometimes the hyenas would heat up pennies with cigarette lighters and toss them to the monkey and laugh like crazy when he screamed.

The big man would stop playing and glare around wildly, shifting his slumping shoulders and making lumpy fists and he would growl and groan like a bear.

I never took sides. In this modern jungle the hyenas' job is to keep the herd clean and vigorous, worried, and always on the alert.

Red Knife never liked to be near the herd, preferring the deeper woods in the back of the park, hunting ducks and geese and squirrels at first dawn, an hour or more before the mounted policeman came riding his rounds. But now the days were so short we hardly saw the sun before it set in the smoke of the city, and this made life hard for everyone except the hyenas who always fed better in darkness, like owls or night hunting cats.

We lived off our snares and nets, saving the powerful crossbow for bigger game. I sewed rabbit skins together and made a curtain for the cave door that kept the warmth of our fire inside and hid any light that might shine out and give our den away.

It was a hard winter for a lot of people, but not for me and Red Knife. We were warm and ate well and kept our spirits harmonious by working through the new snow and touching trees. I learned that some trees are warmer than other trees, the conifers have the warmest blood of all in our domain.

But other people in the herd were suffering because many could find no work and if they didn't work, it was the law of the herd that they should not eat well or be warm, that is: they should suffer.

The herd people could line up for soup or beans to live another day, but I would not because it was taking unfit food from a master that made people slaves. If they killed and counted coup for food, they would not be slaves. They would be stronger. Anyone could figure that out. It was their own personal business to figure it out, each for each.

Those that tried to sleep in the park, or tried to stay awake in the park, froze to death because they didn't know how to live with the land. There were a lot that winter, a lot of old people who had no shelter, no heat, and no food. No one cared and neither did I. The law of the herd is to sacrifice the weak and worn out.

Call the herd system anything you want from Democracy to Capitalism, that's what you get. The rich know this.

Red Knife and I always had a rabbit roasting over the coals, or a squirrel stewing in the iron kettle. We had parched corn, and sometimes we chewed on willow bark because there is something the blood needs in it. I had plenty of time to read about Indians and mountain men.

The more game we ate, the more pelts we had to tan, and before long I had another nice skin robe.

The Russian with the monkey was having just as hard a time as anyone else because the days were so short and the people had no money to share. Once I saw the big man going through a garbage can, feeding the monkey and sneaking a morsel himself when he thought no one was watching.

And once when a crowd of hunger marchers made a protest demonstration through the park, the Mounted Policeman showed what he could do with his horse, the one with the white star on his forehead. I watched from behind the big statue of President Lincoln. With just a touch of the policeman's knee, the horse would shove his shoulders right and left into anybody in the way, bashing them back into the crowd while at the same time the policeman would smack heads with his extra long club.

The Mounted Policeman, a fat and rosy man, had red whiskey in his nose and cheeks, and his horse was fat and shiny, his droppings spattered with undigested corn.

I thought that sometime I would let Red Knife kill that horse and count coup and we would eat well all winter, but it was just a crazy idea because the horse was too big for me to carry to the cave, and the policeman would hunt us down as they did at Wounded Knee.

The Russian wore an old army coat that was too small for him and he carried the monkey inside it next to his heart when they weren't dancing and begging.

The Russian would have been a lot better off in Florida, and he could walk it in a month if he could figure out which direction was south.

He would have been better off eating horsefeed and wearing a

horse blanket. He was the only man I ever felt sorry for. I knew that some terrible herd force had destroyed him while the Great Manitou looked the other way.

It happened late in the day, only a few minutes before cold darkness would freeze down the park. The Russian saw a group of Japanese tourists coming down the sidewalk. He popped out the monkey and the concertina and started singing a strange solemn song, one I'd never heard him play before.

It must have been a famous piece though, because the Japanese stopped and bowed and bowed and bowed again as he played the entire anthem through and the monkey rocked from side to side, shivering in the snow, but doing his part, and when the song was over the Japanese men fetched out Eisenhower dollars and gave them to the monkey and the monkey brought the money to the Russian and he bowed and they bowed and went on down the avenue.

No one except me noticed that pair of hyenas, a male and female of slight build, who saw those metal dollars pass from one hand to the other. The Russian was pleased with his success and had his mouth firmly shut. Knowing the darkness was freezing down, he was ready to go up the street for food and shelter but the hyenas were hungry too.

When he saw them, it was already too late. The woman tossed a coin in the air so the monkey couldn't catch it and lured the monkey away from the Russian and into her hands.

The man went to the Russian and said, Give us the money and you can have the monkey. The big man couldn't understand; his eyes started to roll and his mouth loosened open and a big groan came from deep inside him.

The monkey couldn't figure out what to do. He was too tame or too old to put up a fight. Maybe he thought he'd be better off with the woman.

The big man went after the woman, yelling, Please, please, and the man got behind him and grabbed his coat, but the Russian just clouted him down and went on after the quick-footed woman and the little man got up on his toes like a bullfighter. He looked around and quick as a cat stabbed the Russian in the back. The Russian groaned and swatted the little man again but fell down, slipping on the icy pavement and his own blood. The little man reached inside the coat and took the Eisenhower dollars and snarled at the woman.

She tossed the monkey into a snowbank and they ran down the avenue.

Red Knife said we should go back to the cave and let the Russian freeze or bleed, anything but don't get mixed up with the herd. It isn't worth it, he said. But I'd been watching the Russian a long time and had seen that he wasn't in the herd. He was hardly in the world because somewhere in his past life he had been too badly hurt to ever heal.

If we left, no one would find him until morning.

If we left, he would surely die and the monkey, too.

Red Knife said, it is the Great Manitou that says you live or die, and not for us to say that.

And I said, perhaps the Great Manitou is saying that we should help this once very strong man.

I picked up the monkey who was turning blue and put him inside my robe, and I went to the big Russian and saw that he was alive.

I decided if the Great Manitou could give him strength to lean on me, he would live, and if he did not have the strength, he would die.

Red Knife was greatly agitated that I should give so much of our security away, but I felt the big man deserved a chance.

I told him to lean on me, and lifting him to his feet, half carried him over the shortcuts to the cave. He was still bleeding.

He was groaning but his mouth was shut and his eyes clear. When we came to the cliff I showed him the footholds, and then went ahead and dragged him along behind me into the cave that was warm and comfortable because our fire was still alive.

I gave him the monkey and he collapsed by the fire, his face blue-white and his breath coming in short, raspy gusts.

I took his army coat off and saw two stab wounds in his back. There was nothing I could do except make packs of moss and spiderwebs to stop the bleeding. A little longer and he would have had no more blood to lose.

It seemed to me a very hard piece of work to gain a few Eisenhower dollars.

Old burn scars, front and back, formed a grid, as if someone had barbecued him on one side and when he hadn't said what he was supposed to say, had flipped him over and grilled him on the other. No wonder I mistrust the herd.

Now, Red Knife said, if he lives we must feed him.

Yes, I said, we must.

And Red Knife said, we do not have enough game to feed an injured person.

Perhaps we can eat less and find more food to share.

And Red Knife said, you are in the trap of the herd. The mountain man sees to his own needs first. Let me kill him and count coup.

Red Knife and I have never quarreled, never even disagreed before. He was more than a brother to me, he was my right arm and my teacher, the pure other half of myself. Still, I couldn't let the big man die.

Let me think. Give me some time to clear my mind, I asked Red Knife, and he looked at me with slit eyes like I was crazy, but he didn't argue anymore.

He sat in the shadows and stared into the fire, and the cave was silent except for the raspy breathing of the Russian.

A little blood bubbled on his loose lower lip, and I guessed one of his lungs had been cut. It all depended on how badly it was cut and how strong the big man was.

Probably he would die and we would not have to decide to kill him. I wished we could keep our paths straight and simple, but this was not straight nor was it simple. If he lived we would need to keep him until spring, and we would have to decide how to erase the cave memory from his mind. He must never be allowed to come back or tell anyone about the cave.

Then I let the Great Manitou decide whether he lived or died.

In two days blood no longer bubbled on his lip. His eyes were open but he was smart enough not to move and open up his wounds or maybe he was just too weak. A blizzard locked up the park. No one could survive the cold and the wind and ice that piled upon the trees and electric wires and broke them.

It was the worst storm Red Knife had ever seen. We couldn't

catch any game and all we had to eat was parched corn. It was a time when you live off your autumn fat. There was no singing of birds. Even if we hadn't a wounded man to feed, we would have been forced to think of finding meat. We had plenty of time to think and plan.

We waited until moondown and the snow was falling hard enough to hide our tracks. Taking along a piece of rope, Red Knife and I ran across the park, avoiding the sidewalks. Red Knife stopped once and said, Listen! I heard the trees moaning with their unbearable loads of ice, like deer dying under the weight and teeth of the lion.

It was a bad night for all living things. All you could do was set your teeth and bear it, or attack, as Red Knife and I were doing. We did not believe we could survive the cold winter very long.

And that is why we loped in long strides through the shadows and glare of ice and crunchy frozen snow.

We were at the station in a short time, but there we had to wait and scout patiently. We had to set our teeth and endure the pain of the cold so that we could plunder and count coup.

We could see the policemen sitting by a heater with their coats off. They were watching the picture and listening to the picture. They had taken off their leather puttees. They were not going anywhere until morning.

We trotted from that grey building down the path to the stables and scouted the barn and feedroom. We stayed in the shadows and moved quietly as snow on snow. There was no one there.

Only the horses were in their warm stalls, standing knee deep

in fresh straw, munching on baskets of alfalfa hay or nuzzling feed boxes for corn.

There were several fat horses. Each one wore a halter and a blanket. Oh, I thought, how I would like to live on the prairie and carry a feathered lance and ride my own feathered horse, but I knew it was only a wish. I lived in a place where your life depends on your not being seen.

I picked the horse with the white star on his forehead, the one the policeman liked to lunge into the people with. I picked him because I remembered him. If I am not in any man's memory, then I am safe. So this horse was chosen to go.

I gave him a handful of corn and knotted my rope to his halter, opened his stall and led him outside, carefully closing all the doors.

He followed right along as we loped back across the park. All our tracks and traces would be buried soon by the snowfall. He was a well-trained horse and memorable for his lunging shoulders and flicking front hooves.

He was a good horse for his job, but he was also a horse meant to be stolen and butchered by me and Red Knife. Perhaps the Great Manitou said that. Perhaps it was only because he was memorable.

Deep in the grove of spruce trees near the cave, we stopped and Red Knife took the crossbow and shot the horse right through the white star on his forehead with a rebar, and counted coup, and then I took my butcher knife and skinned in the starlight.

By dawn the horsehide was folded into a bundle and hidden under a spruce tree where it would stay frozen until spring. The

meaty parts of the legs were cached up high and hidden in the biggest spruce tree, and the meat of the loin and back I carried to the cave.

Snow had already covered the blood, and the hulk of bones was slowly disappearing. If I needed meaty bones I could come back so long as the cold locked up the park. I planned to feed the bones to the lions whenever I could.

I climbed into the cave for the last time in the gray light of daybreak and looked through the falling snow at the ground we had traveled in the night and there was not a dimple to betray us.

The horse was gone. The police would make it disappear in the inventory and another horse would be quietly moved in. They would not even look very hard for fear that the public might learn of the unaccountable horse and they would be disgraced as victims of superior stealth and strength.

The Russian grew stronger from the rich soup and roasted meat I fed him. The monkey lived off my cache of peanuts.

Red Knife sat in the shadows staring into the fire. The monkey was the only one except me who knew he was there and he was afraid of Red Knife because he knew Red Knife wanted to kill him and count coup.

But so long as I did not speak against the big man and the monkey, Red Knife accepted my ruling and abided by the fire.

And though the big man had a rumbling cough deep in his chest, he could move around and go outside to do his functions and he had sense enough not to wander around, but to come back to the cave and quietly wait for spring.

The horsemeat stayed frozen in the dark grove of spruce.

When we needed more, I'd climb into the tree and hack off a chunk.

Except for Red Knife worrying about the Russian betraying us, it was a quiet hibernating winter, comfortable enough for any mountain man.

Red Knife didn't understand that the big man couldn't get his brain working good enough to betray us even if he wanted to. He'd been tortured and burned too much.

He usually only spoke two words and usually got them backwards. They were 'please' and 'thank you'. He had a few other words but they never fit anywhere. One was 'amazing' and another was 'brotherhood'.

Usually he said nothing but sometimes played the concertina and sort of hummed a music I didn't always know. He knew Mexicali Rose pretty good.

When spring came, I salted the leftover meat and buried the white starred horsehead in the grove of spruce. That day we were able to catch a tasty young rabbit. Soon the ponds would be free of ice and the ducks and geese would return.

But Red Knife never changed. He sat by the fire looking into the glowing coals as if he were looking into the eye of the Great Manitou.

One morning when I was preparing the horsehide for tanning, using the ashes of the winter's fire and the fat from the horse's own well-fed body, the big man looked out the cave entrance at the grey and barelimbed park, wet now with melting slush, but with a brilliant sun reflecting in jagged splashes of orange, and he came back to the fire, the same fire-eye that Red Knife stared at,

and he said to the fiery eye, 'Amazing. Thank you.' And then he
picked up his concertina and put the monkey inside his coat, went
to the doorway and looked at the sun with longing. Then he came
back, wrapped his big arms around me in a big bear hug and with
a strange, distorted look of sorrow on his face he said in a cracking
voice, as plainly as he could, 'Please'.

I'd been hoping he would not only recover from his stab
wounds, but also from that torture of an earlier time, but when I
looked into his eyes, I saw a burnt kernel of corn, too damaged to
ever sprout a new life.

That afternoon he played the concertina in the sunshine near
the avenue. Red Knife and me strolled through the weeping trees
where a few little birds sang. Red Knife worried that the Russian
would betray us, and I told him that was the least of our worries.

TRAPS

O
UTSIDE CENTRAL PARK, the city cackled and screamed
with all the female insanity of an overcrowded egg
ranch, but inside on Stuyvesant Pond ducks cruised over
the still water with their newborn in tow, and a blue heron
perched on one leg, held at point, waited for the flash of a minnow
in the shallows. Staying more toward the island in the center of
the pond a pair of white swans, their great wings tucked in crisply,
their slender necks curved as if they'd been formed by slow-
moving currents of water, worked through the tranquil pond like
a pair of royal galleons convoying their brood of four unfledged
cygnets.

Red Knife and me watched from a covert of tall marsh grass.

"We need a couple of those fat babies," Red Knife whispered,
staring at the smaller white birds that rode the water under the
protection of their imperious parents.

Spitted over a slow hardwood fire, they'd make mighty fine

belly-packing material, I thought, but even without the Park patrols, bagging a couple of young swans would not be easy. Their nesting ground on the swampy island stood secure as a castle surrounded by a moat. The water looked deep and black.

The mallards were more foolish, swimming carelessly close to the shore reeds where all kinds of hungry hunters could be waiting. There were so many ducks, they could afford to lose a few, but the swans had none to spare.

"We can build a raft," I told Red Knife. "We can go over in the night and take them while they sleep."

I suddenly felt the presence of a stranger, and dropped to one knee, scanning the surrounding trees for a gamekeeper or gardener, but nothing showed, nothing moved. It worried me. I'd caught that feeling several times in the past month and I trusted my senses more than a guidebook or a newspaper.

Red Knife knew what I felt. "Something is spying on us again," he agreed, but we needed to know what and why.

We gathered a few broken logs from a beech grove close by and bound them together with bittersweet vine. We hid the raft in the tall grass close to the water and went back to camp to wait for nightfall. In the darkness we would stuff the young swans into a gunny sack before they could shriek a warning. Reading a biography of Sacajaweah, I drowsed on my bearskin and as always, when I sleep, Red Knife goes somewhere else. When I awaken he is always there by my side, even if no one else can see him.

I awakened about dark. Red Knife leaned against a log, waiting patiently.

Darkness never really comes down on the park because the city lights surround it like a nimbus, washing out stars and moon. Still

a heartache dream floated through the trees and over the gardens like the fumes of spring.

The patrols leave when the day changes to night, and the swans tuck their heads under their wings to shut out the rosy embers of the city.

Wearing only moccasins and loincloths, we carefully worked our way through the woods to the Pond. When I sensed the stranger close by, I felt the big knife at my side just to be sure. Red Knife touched my arm, telling me to go slower, to make a proper stalk even though we'd been here just a few hours before.

We reached the swampgrass and snaked our way to the spot where we'd cached the raft.

No raft. No trace. Not a mark in the grass leading anywhere. We would roast no fat young swans this night.

I don't know if I was more angered than worried. I had fasted for this hunt and when Red Knife and I returned to camp, we had to eat cold carp fried the day before.

"It is the stranger who has humbled us," Red Knife said. "We must kill him."

"For sure," I nodded. It was a vexing problem because the stranger knew who we were but we knew nothing.

I am a mountain man, not Buck Rogers. I respect the memories of Jim Bridger and my namesake Kit Carson, not some sci-fi comic strip superman, product of a sick, citified imagination. I live off the land and fear nothing. It is not an easy life, but it is as pure and natural as I can make it in these times.

"It leaves no tracks," Red Knife muttered gloomily. "Maybe it is the ghost of the bear we killed last Christmas."

"We must find it and kill it," I said.

"You have to see it first," Red Knife shook his great head. "My medicine is not strong enough."

"We know when it's close by."

"Its medicine is stronger than mine." Red Knife said, sinking into a black mood, as if he were preparing for his own fated death.

"Let's build another raft, but this time we use it for bait. We hide and kill him when he steals the raft."

"It knows where we are all the time. You can not hide from the watcher."

"Then let's build another raft and stay with it. Make it come out and fight."

"It will sink the raft in the pond and we can not swim."

"Red Knife, my brother," I said, "I do not intend to eat cold carp forever and I am not ready to turn tail like a yeller dog."

We went to sleep growling at each other and settling nothing. I'd never seen Red Knife give up so easily.

Our summer camp is on a little knoll in the south side of the park which has gone back to the wild. The undergrowth around the knoll is so thick with briars and vines, no one comes near and we can build a small cook fire without worrying about someone smelling smoke. Off to one side is a giant silver barked sycamore tree that shades the knoll in the bee droning afternoons. It is a perfect place for outdoor living.

We had our morning herbal tea and blackberries with some johnny cakes for breakfast. I put the bearskin on a bush to air out and tidied up the camp. Red Knife was no help.

I started to hone my knife when I felt the little prickle like electricity on the back of my neck.

"It's coming," I whispered.

"I knew it would find us." If Red Knife could have turned pale he'd have been white as a Swede. "Its medicine is too strong."

I loaded the crossbow with a steel rebar. The crossbow, made from a car spring and some other junk has more killing power than a Sharps fifty buffalo rifle. I meant to have a fight.

"You are letting your superstitions defeat you," I told Red Knife. "There is an answer to everything."

The presence came slowly closer, slipping through the briars like a cat. I couldn't see it in the undergrowth but the prickle on my neck was fearsome.

"Get ready, Red Knife. We're going to have it out this time."

"We are already lost. We are in its power."

I felt like kicking him. Always before in tight places he's been cool as a cave. Now he was so cool he was frozen.

The invisible stranger stopped. It stayed somewhere in the trees where it could look into our camp. I studied every limb and leaf and could see nothing unusual.

"You out there," I yelled, crazy with frustration. "What do you want?"

No answer. Not even a breeze to stir the silver and green leaves.

"You want to fight?"

Nothing.

"Pow-wow?"

No response from the wall of flickering green.

"It is a ghost," Red Knife said. "It is here not to fight but to haunt us all the rest of our days."

"Yeller dog!" I yelled into the greenness. I turned slowly in a circle, facing the greenness, keeping the heavy steel crossbow at the ready. I had extra steel rebars in my quiver ready to reload.

"Ya water-bellied skunk-sucker!"

I was as mad as I was scared. Nobody has ever pushed me around yet.

"Come on out and I'll whip you threadbare!"

The leaves rippled on a vagrant breeze but no one replied, no one appeared.

"I'll show you something!" I yelled again, and quick aimed at the massive trunk of the sycamore, touched the trigger and drove the three foot rebar half way into the tree. Sap the color of blood spurted from the wound.

I whipped another rebar out of the shoulder quiver but before I could reload a voice came from behind me. "Now you've gone and done it, you big creep!"

A queer fine voice, a clear voice, a girl's voice.

I turned to see her standing in the clearing, her arms crossed over her chest, her feet set solidly apart as if she didn't intend to be moved either forward or backward.

I eyed her and carefully slipped the rebar into its slot and cranked back the spring.

Her green eyes glittered dangerously and her hair fell like a silver waterfall misting down past her shoulders. Her mouth wasn't so pretty because she'd set it in a hostile line.

"Kill her, Kit," Red Knife whispered. "Quick!"

"Oh, put that stupid thing away. You've just maimed a really beautiful tree. What would your mother say?" She glared at me.

I couldn't tell her that Red Knife put a rebar through my flipperty-flopperty mother's head because she meant to lock us up. "My mother is my business," I said. "Who are you?"

I cranked the crossbow back to neutral.

"My name in Sycamore Spring and I live here in Central Park."

"We were here first," I said. "We've been here almost a year now."

"So?" she challenged.

"So leave us alone. You took our raft, didn't you?"

"I sure did," she snapped. "You were going to kill the cygnets."

"We hunt our game our own way."

"You can change your ways," she said.

"Not for you," I said, thinking that no matter how pretty she looked in army fatigues, she wasn't going to run my life for me.

"If you're going to kill and maim everything in sight, why don't you go back to where you came from?" She took a step forward but I didn't back off.

"We eat what we kill. We don't waste anything. We live the life of self-sufficient mountain men."

"You'd even eat those baby swans."

"Darn right," I growled. "We worked hard on that raft."

Her voice changed to something you might call patient reasonableness. Her eyes set their green glow into mine and I felt something different than the prickling on the back of my neck. "There are enough cripples, enough over-aged, enough over-crowded, but those cygnets are not any of those. You understand, they're precious."

"Precious to us," I grinned, and her expression suddenly shifted

into a thundercloud again, lightning forking out of the green fire.

You're hopeless. For you it's kill, kill, kill. For you it's stupid, stupid, stupid. OK. OK.," she said with some finality. "You'll see."

Even if I'd wanted to stop her or shoot her, she moved too quickly. She moved with the grace of a green racer, and in a second she blended into the trees and out of sight.

"Wait!" I yelled, "Wait, let's talk!" But I could feel her disappearing, withdrawing farther and farther away.

I threw the crossbow down and walked a slow circle around camp, trying to assimilate the new complexity.

"You had your chance," Red Knife said dismally.

"Don't tell me that again," I said. "She'll be back. I know she'll be back."

"I hope not," Red Knife said.

"But who is she?" I murmured. "What is a pretty girl in army clothes doing here in the Park? Why? How? It doesn't make any sense."

"Do we make any sense?"

"No," I had to laugh. "None at all. But we know how to live off the land."

In the afternoon, we went out to check our snares and traps. Almost always, if we work at it, we'll find a nice fat rabbit in a snare, but today the snares had all been turned out of the tiny animal runs except for one which held an aged jackrabbit.

Still, it was all we had. We reset the snares and dressed the old rabbit and put him in the iron kettle to stew his gristle into jelly. At best he'd make a strong soup if we could find some wild leeks and dandelions to add to it.

My mind was so mixed up I couldn't tell up from down. We'd had such a simple, easy life for so long, it didn't take much of a problem to turn it all topsy-turvy. The memory of the meeting with the girl named Sycamore kept running and running through my head. I felt as if I'd behaved like a kid or a hayseed. I went over to the rebar that I'd driven into the tree and tried to pull it out, but it would stay there for the life of the tree, an indissolvable union. A bloody sap oozed from the wound, staining the silver patched bark. I felt sorry I'd done it, but then I grew sick of my weakness and hung my fur cap with the foxtail from the iron peg just to show I didn't give a darn, could even make a joke of it. "Get smart with me tree and I'll make you look like an iron porky-pine!"

We didn't see her next day, but our traps were sprung and empty. We had to dig into our cache of pemmican for supper, and that's hard times.

Next day early we went to the pond and caught a duck with a fish line baited with a doughball. I'd rather have had a nice cottontail or squirrel, but a mountain man takes what he can get. A mountain man don't like creases in his belly. It riles him up some.

Red Knife wouldn't talk. His long face said "doom, doom, doom," because he believed her medicine was stronger than his.

Usually we are of one mind and purpose, but now I could hardly get him moving. Maybe he was smarter than I give him credit for, but surviving is never easy, and carrying a dependent is too hard.

"Red Knife," I said, "She will go away like the spring time or the wind."

"No," he groaned, "Every day she grows stronger."

"Let's go to the little zoo tonight and catch us a nice fat lamb," I said, to divert him from dark thoughts and encourage him back to our old easy going days.

"We will fail," Red Knife said. "She will find a way."

"Not if she doesn't know," I said. "We'll leave camp after dark like we were going over to the Theatre for squabs, but at the ravine we'll sidle into the oaks and be over the fence before she can guess what we're up to."

He shook his head glumly, but I was determined to have a decent meal for a change.

Long past midnight, I listened and sharpened my senses, but I felt none of the warnings that Sycamore was close by.

We moved out silently, following a little trail by the light of the ever-burning, oscillating city. My feelings were good. We were finally doing something that challenged our woodcraft and our hunting code. It is not easy to slip into a guarded sheep pen and come out with a fat lamb under your arm.

Adventure cleans out your blood.

Coming to a surfaced path, we walked along easy as pie, but coming to a foot bridge we moved off, eased down to the bottom of the ravine and followed it upstream and still I felt no alien vibrations. We traveled a mile out of our way to get to the fence without Sycamore's knowledge or interference.

The chain link fence stood low enough to let the children see in, but high enough to keep the sheep from jumping out. Floodlights made the pen as bright as day, and you never knew exactly when the night patrol would come by.

To get into the shed where the sheep slept, we had to slip over the fence and stay in its latticed shadow, slowly and inconspicuously creep to the shed, quietly open the door and slip inside. Then usually you would work your way through the sleeping flock, select your lamb, boost him into a seated position in the crook of your arm so that he won't blat or struggle, and depart.

We searched the rank smelling shed and came up with nothing. Off in the grass I heard them blatting. They'd been turned loose out on the lawn. We'd not come prepared to hunt, and we went back to camp empty-handed.

Humbled and bitter, I tried to lay it on the girl but it was my fault for not scouting the pen in the afternoon to be sure the sheep were there. My mistake and no one else's. Red Knife kept his thoughts to himself. I tripped over a vine and jammed my thumb and cursed the bad luck that had fallen upon us.

As we came closer to camp, I began to feel the presence. She was hanging around close by. She watched us returning in defeat.

We entered our clearing on the knoll and I heard her laughing off in the darkness. It was a silly giggle, but I took it as a taunt or an insult. She could see we were empty-handed and tired, but still her laughter rippled out of the woods.

I lost my temper. "By dang you woman!" I yelled. "I'll split you, split you crown to crotch, nape to notch, I promise!"

Whether she heard me or not, I don't know for when I had gotten my senses back, there was no sound of her in the darkness.

I went to my bearskin to lie down and found a garland of daisies and Sweet Williams on my pillow.

Red Knife had nothing to say and only gloom in his eyes. I felt

a kind of sorrow or regret. Maybe she hadn't been laughing at our failure, maybe she'd made a little friendly joke. I felt we were in the grip of larger forces and I don't even believe in larger forces. There is no force bigger than me so long as I don't depend on anything or anybody.

I decided that all this had to be settled once and for all and right soon. I had to catch her and either kill her or make a good enough threat to run her off. There was no other way we could live comfortably in the park, and I reminded myself, we came here first. We had pioneered the sneaky fishing, the poaching of gamebirds, the extravagantly contrived slaughter of horse and bear.

"Put your mind to work, Red Knife," I said. "We have to catch that girl."

"I wish to take her scalp and count coup." Red Knife said.

"Maybe we can talk her into leaving us alone."

"Are you afraid of a squaw?"

"It's not that." I muttered.

"You don't want her silver hair?"

"All I want is for her to leave us be."

"Her medicine is too strong. She will divide us and make us her dogs."

I felt the flowers against my cheek and smelled the spicy Sweet Williams. I wanted then so much to just talk to her without any pressure or stresses. I wanted to touch her hand, touch her face the way the flowers touched mine.

In the morning I circled the camp five times before I found an oak tree on the fringe of camp which showed a scratch in the

lichen covered trunk, and on up in the branches I found a long silver hair.

At least I knew her roost. Hoping she'd come back I put one of my best egret feathers in the crotch.

Red Knife and me took our fishing line and went over to the fountain where the big trout loaf. I spread my blanket by the pool and pretended to read a book. As soon as the cop passed by and no one was looking, I flipped my grub-baited hook into the pool, felt the tug, and gave the fish a mighty jerk that brought him sailing right into my lap. In half a second I had him wrapped up in the blanket and Red Knife and me strolled back towards the woods for lunch.

If you keep it simple as well as incredible, it's easy.

The big trout and a heap of wild purslane improved our moods considerably. The heck with the fat lamb. We'd take care of that matter next week.

"Tonight we go to the Greek Theatre and fetch back a few squabs." I suggested.

"That girl?" Red Knife couldn't forget our defeat.

"With all the pigeons in the park, I don't think she'd mind."

"It is no way to live having to hunt on the command of a squaw."

"We're going to do something about that, too."

Just before dark, I went to Sycamore's roost and saw that the white feather was gone. In its place lay a handful of wild plums.

I had her hooked!

We had no trouble gathering the squabs. You only have to climb up into the eaves of the Theatre and reach into the different

nests until you find the birds you want. They don't know what's happening to them in the dark. We only wanted half a dozen, two to eat right away and the rest to salt and smoke.

That solved our food problem for awhile no matter what Sycamore did.

In the morning I put a flat chalcedony pebble in the crotch of the tree and while I was there I planned my trap.

I had to catch her and talk to her face to face. Somehow I wasn't sure what to talk about. Deep down I guess I wanted to know if we could settle our differences and end up friends. I didn't really know what a friend was. Red Knife was a lot more than that.

In the afternoon I found the stone gone and in its place was a canna leaf, rolled up into a horn and it was full of wild strawberries. Nothing like this had ever happened to me in my whole life. I felt a stirring somewhere in my chest. What was it? It was too confusing. Somehow I wanted to protect her and somehow I wanted her out of my life.

I had to trap her and get it straight.

In the morning I put my skull ring with the red glass eyes in the crotch of the tree, and laid a noose under the duff, running the end over to a sapling birch I'd bent over and set on a trigger that would snap when she brushed against it. I checked it all out twice, making sure that nothing at all appeared to be disturbed.

I waited in camp all day listening for her to yell when the snare grabbed her feet and hauled her up. My woods sense seemed to tell me she was close by but I wasn't sure.

Late in the afternoon I decided something had gone wrong and I circled around the big oak. The trap wasn't sprung. Red Knife shook his head, telling me to be careful. I came up on the opposite

side of the oak to see if she'd taken my ring. I had to lean over a dead branch to see into the crotch and even as I touched it, I knew my mistake. Before I could react, my ankles were seized and in no time I was hanging upside down. Red Knife stood frozen. Quick as I could figure, I pulled my big knife and cut the rope. I landed on my shoulder and bounced to my feet, the knife at the ready.

"What's the matter with you?" she demanded, stepping out in the open. "If you want to talk, you don't have to try to trap me like an animal."

"How'd you catch on?" I growled.

"The trees are on my side. Now what do you want?"

I stopped to look at her before I spoke. I'd been doing some dumb things and I had to change my ways. She was, I guess you'd say, pretty as a picture. I mean she stood tall and easy, not afraid, or worried, or beaten down. And when I looked in her green eyes, I thought my breastbone was rendering down to lard.

"I wanted to talk, but you always stayed out of range."

"The way I heard it, I was supposed to stay out of range or get split from crown to. . ." She smiled.

I blushed and thought what a crazy fool I was.

"What do you want to talk about?"

"Well, me and my friend Red Knife have to hunt to eat. And if you get in our way, it makes it harder for us."

"I told you if you'd just take the cripples and cull out the older game, you'd be doing everyone a favor."

"A snare don't know how to guess the age of a rabbit."

"Sure it does. If you set it high you'll catch the old ones, you set it low you catch the young ones."

Possible. I just hadn't thought about it.

"Do you eat meat?" I slipped my knife back in its sheath.

"No. I don't need to."

I took a step forward and she didn't step back. I didn't know what I was doing. Over her shoulder I could see Red Knife wearing his saddest expression. He was shaking his head, no, no, no. . . .

I took another step and put my hand on her arm. We were both brown, but she was golden and I was dirty. I hated myself there for a second. I couldn't speak.

"What is it, Kit?" she asked quietly.

"Honest, Sycamore, I just don't know. I feel such a power tearing my insides apart I figured if I touched you it'd all settle down."

"At least you're not mad anymore," she murmured. "I think I'd better go.

"Please don't," I said. "There's still a lot I need to know."

"There's nothing to me. I live with the trees, that's all. I come from a place called Briarcliff, and I and the trees get along fine."

"But what about the winter?"

"Last winter I worked in a hothouse."

"We lived in a cave not too far from here," I said.

Red Knife made a horrendous face. He didn't want anyone to know about our cave.

"I can't see Red Knife," she said, "but I can feel that he's close by. He must be a fine man to be your companion."

Red Knife face changed. He was thinking.

"Oh, he gets a little gnarly once in awhile," I laughed, teasing Red Knife.

"You should count your blessings. Good friends are scarce," she said. "I know because even with the trees I feel a bit lonely once in awhile."

"You want to come see our camp?"

"Why not?" and she smiled with such a sweet warmth I about fell down backwards.

We walked into camp, and I tried to cover up some of the grease spots and such, but she paid my housekeeping no mind.

"Would you like some wild raspberry tea?" I asked, trying to be polite.

"Sure," she said. "Did Red Knife teach you that?"

"Maybe he did. He sure taught me a lot," I said, poking up the coals and putting on the iron kettle.

"I didn't have a teacher. I always ran from teachers. I guess the trees taught me everything I know."

It had been so long since I'd talked to anyone except Red Knife I barely managed a conversation, but for some reason we didn't seem to need a lot of palaver to pass back and forth. There was another kind of an invisible telephone line between me and her.

"Time to go," she said, and I could hardly believe my ears.

"What...?" I stuttered. "Why...?"

I'd not thought of her leaving, hadn't asked her to. Where did she get such a nutty idea?"

She stood tall and shapely as a pine tree, and I couldn't think of what to say. Did I want her to move in? What would I do with her?

"Where are you going?" I stammered.

"The lilacs are blooming. I love to come in on them at evening time."

"When am I going to see you again?"

"Don't set a trap," she giggled like a little girl, her green eyes all merry and little lights dancing in them.

"I grabbed ahold of her hand. "Look," I said, "I'm a mountain man and we speak only a few chosen words."

That sounded fine but I didn't have the chosen words. I felt like a greenhorn that can't let loose of the bear.

She waited for me to say something and then she saw I couldn't say it, so she just leaned over and said, "I'll be back," and kissed me and turned around and in a second she was gone into the trees.

"You are in her trap," Red Knife said.

"Now look here," I said right back at him. "She may be a bit forward, but she's good people and you got no call to run her down."

Red Knife wisely kept silent. He looked off at the iron bar sticking in the sycamore tree.

"Red Knife," I felt a crazy happy excitement as it suddenly hit me. There was no need for me to feel that aching desolation in my chest anymore. "Red Knife, she said she'd be back!"

He slowly shook his noble head with a meaning I didn't bother to understand. Bedazzled by a new world full of blooming flowers and sunbursts of colored, singing birds, I felt like flying.

FEAR

REDKNIFE WARNED ME. In his quiet voice with the texture of granite, he said, "Kit, we are too many to camp here so long."

It was early summer. I was a new husband and I squandered my fighting energy like a bee tumbling in a red rose, lazy and happy.

It is never very hard to live in Central Park. There are so many places to hide and so many good things to eat, it is a very happy life unless our desires become unreal. If we attempted to live high on the hog, dress like dandies and strut down the streets, we couldn't survive. But if we are satisfied with simple Goodwill clothing and eat ducks and lambs, trout and bear, we live very well.

I have been married only two moons, using our time.

Sycamore cannot see Red Knife, but she has the extra sense perception to know where he is and more and more he becomes revealed to her. She can talk to him now if she wishes but she doesn't always understand his reply.

63

For a long time Red Knife couldn't understand why I needed Sycamore, why I changed, and then he realized I needed a woman and she was as good as any. Now he is discreet and tactful, and fades away when we want to be alone.

And I couldn't understand why we should move summer camp now. We built only the smallest of fires for cooking, using dry hardwood, and our stores were kept in the shade of a big old pine tree, and our bearskin bed was nearby in the open where we could awaken once in awhile and watch the moon. You cannot see any stars inside the city. Most of our goods were stored in the cave in the bluffs.

Sycamore and I were standing by an old statue of a general who was once thought to be a very great man because his troops suffered so many casualties and yet continued on in their faith in his genius.

I said, "He was a genius at killing off his men. He could create death better than anyone else."

"How do you know?" Sycamore asked.

"In the winter I go to the Carnegie Library and read history. Why are you looking so peaked?"

"It's nothing. The air here is bad. We should move west."

"I would like to move out west, but we are on an island and I cannot drive a car."

"I know. I am not complaining," she whispered.

"We must think of this. There must be some way to move out west," I said, deciding to make a plan. A mountain man can do anything if he keeps his mind on it.

From the north I heard the crashing of underbrush, the thumping of hooves, the angry shout of a man.

"Clear the camp," I said to Sycamore, and with Red Knife beside me ran toward the oncoming blundering beast.

A horse, handsome and shiny as if waxed, carrying the saddle of the Mounted Park Police, came right at me, its eyes bulging with fear and its neck running with sweat. When it saw me coming, it stopped, reared, spun on its hind legs and thundered back the way it had come.

"That was close," I said to Red Knife.

"Another minute and the horse and its lost rider would have taken us," Red Knife agreed.

I could see a tinge of sadness and anxiety color his somber features. He knew as well as I did that we were very close to being caught and our goods destroyed by the savages.

Returning to the clearing we found it empty as if no human being had ever been there. I knew she was in a tree where she would feel safe. I whistled a bob-white call and heard a dove coo in return, and in a moment she was beside me.

"This place is still as good as any," I said, "but we're going to have to be more alert."

That night I looked into the glowing embers of our tiny fire and tried to think of a way off the island. If we could just get into mountains; if we could find a National Park. But first we had to escape the island.

Thoughts of the devilment those savages outside might think up for us if we were ever taken crowded my mind and spurred my thoughts toward freedom.

In the night I dreamed of the horse running toward me, rearing and running the other way. It was a powerful dream and I told it to Red Knife in the morning.

"Horses," he said.

"What?"

"We could escape on horses."

It seemed impossible. Two horses with mountain people riding would stick out more than if we were just walking.

"When the Great Manitou sends you a vision, you must accept the instructions."

I rarely argue with Red Knife because he is almost always right. The only time he's been wrong was when he wanted to kill Sycamore.

"What do you think?" I asked Sycamore, because my wife is my partner.

"Let me think. Something is in the back of my head."

"While you are thinking, Red Knife and I will scout the police stables."

"We already know them well enough."

Red Knife actually smiled as he remembered the time we stole a fat horse from the stable during the Great Blizzard.

We left the car spring crossbow in camp, carrying only the long knife.

"There will be no blizzard to hide us this time," I said, leading the way through the back trails across the park toward the Park Station. I was thinking that we were pushing our luck.

We came in from the rear of the old building built of stone. They did not bother with landscaping the area and we had plenty of cover.

There were old trees and many vines and all kinds of high bushes and low bushes crowding each other. It should have been

easy enough to scout from there. Once we worked around to the front, there would be extreme danger, but we planned to retreat immediately to this area and disappear in the thick undergrowth and forest beyond. You have to plan for any kind of bad luck. Even then it is not enough.

We memorized the trees and checked the trails of small animals, but it was very thick brush and deer did not even pass through it. We stayed there an hour or more but we could see nothing except a storeroom which had one window.

We moved slowly toward the side where the stable doors were made of thick planks, big enough for trucks to enter with hay and leave with manure. Deep inside, the horses waited in their stalls to be saddled and ridden on patrol through the park.

The police headquarters were in the front of the building and the storeroom fitted in between the headquarters as we tried to view the front where the policemen came and went.

I noticed that they showed signs of long years of drink and wore the artificial air of men who know they are betraying their life and so put on a coat of paint that says they are being of service to mankind. We all know that look. It is the look of the painted harlot.

I smelled the vomit but I couldn't relate it to our mission or the place. We passed it by. A mistake. Whenever something is where it is not supposed to be, you must scout it very carefully even if you find only the puke of a dog.

We settled into covert and counted policemen coming in and out the door. We counted them riding in and others riding out. We tried to understand those in charge and those who were beginners. We tried to imagine escape routes.

To steal a horse in a blizzard is easy. Especially if you eat the horse and all the sign of the animal's existence have been covered by snow, but to steal two horses in early summer is not so easy.

Yes, we could probably steal the horses out of the big doors in the night, but then what? A horse is a hard animal to hide.

I did not think much of our chances, and when one lives wild, one must always succeed. Cripples die quickly in the wild, as well as careless ones.

We heard him too late. A big man with a red face. His tunic was undone and his eyes half crazed. He did not reach for his club or gun, he simply lunged at me. I dodged and he stumbled but did not fall. Red Knife and I ran hard for the cover in the back of the building and I dived into the thick brush thinking I'd found safety, but I was netted in vines. I could not move swiftly, and struggling away, I opened up the path for my enemy.

Suddenly the vines gave way and I dropped into a well or a root cellar. Whatever it had been, it was a pit for me, clogged with vines that restrained the swiftness I needed most.

Red Knife vanished in the confusion. The policeman leaped on me and before I could kick or bite, he had his big arm around my neck with a choke hold. The darkness came immediately. I was taken by the savages.

"I think he's dead. I think you broke his neck," I heard from the darkness. I kept my eyes closed, trying to learn what had happened to me. "You are in deep shit, man. This is the third one and I don't think you got a chance of coming out clean."

"That sleeper hold is straight from the academy," another voice said, a rougher voice.

I tried to place them. The first one was either a southerner or a black man. He was not the senior. He was either young or black. I decided he must be older and black, which made him still the inferior in rank.

"You do have to drink your whiskey out of a bottle and then you do kind of forget what you ever learned about control in the academy."

"He's still breathing."

"Then why you got him back in here?"

"I thought he was about dead. Now I think he'll come out of it."

"Come out of it in a coma."

"Coma, hell. If it's a coma he's goin' to come out of it six feet under and no questions asked."

"How come they pair me with you, Micky? Why me with you?"

"Because we're both undesireables, if you know what I mean."

"Lordy yes, I do know what you mean."

I could feel the steel on my wrist. Handcuffed to an iron pipe. The steel clamped tightly on my wrist. I could never slip my hand through. I kept my eyes closed, hoping they would go away.

"You goin' to tell the sarge?"

"Hell no, and you neither. If this weirdo wakes up, we take him out to the football field and kick his ass clear out of the Park."

"And if he don't?"

"Quit worryin'. You're doin' it on purpose, tryin' to stick the needle in my head and I'm about to lose my temper and if you want the rumpus to begin you just keep stickin' me."

"Take it easy, Micky. We partners, y'know."

They walked away. A door closed. I waited several minutes

before I opened my eyes. I was not in the stable. It could not be in the headquarters because they couldn't hide me there. If I was not in the stable or headquarters then I was either in another building or I was in the storeroom.

I could smell the sweet fragrance of alfalfa hay as well as the strong aroma of confined horses.

I tried to be calm and analytical. They had hurt me, and they wanted no more trouble.

I was manacled close to the floor. I could lie down or sit up but nothing else. It was dark, lighted only by the one window admitting the grey light of the city. After a time I could see old desks piled on one wall, cardboard boxes and broken chairs. Yes, I knew then where I was and where the window was.

I licked my hand and tried to slip through the steel bracelet, at the same time using all my willpower to keep calm. I had never been handcuffed or imprisoned in my whole life and now I was taken by the savages. The more I tried to pull my hand through the steel the more my thoughts blurred and my resolve for calm faded.

Where was Red Knife? Sycamore?

Lightning rolled around in my head like coils of barbed wire.

I had to get loose!

Black clouds roiled and crashed inside my head and the lightning bolts struck at each other like rattlesnakes.

Freedom!

I'd have screamed except it would make it worse.

I put both feet against the stanchion and tried to break it loose from the ceiling with brute strength but there wasn't the slightest give to the iron pipe.

I jerked as hard as I could and only hurt my hand all the more.

The black clouds boiled with silver and iron grey edges scraping each other raw and cracking out the serpentine barbs of lightning in my mind, crashing and thrashing black and silver clouds erupting in my mind.

And then like a poison the fear went into my bloodstream and streaked through my nerves, barbed greyhounds streaking through every cell in my body, alerting every sense to the catastrophe, telegraphing the call to battle stations, each part of the body called upon for the supreme effort and supreme sacrifice, however it was decided, because what was at stake was freedom and in that word for me was the word survival. I am a mountain man. I could never be a locked-up person, meek and mild. O no!

There would be no help, no allies, no luck. Whatever was to be done, would be done by my entire person inflamed with fear. Fear, not cowardice. Two different things.

I'd snared enough small animals to see the fear but not cowardice in their eyes, and I'd seen the ultimate desperate gathering of the body forces to crash out for freedom.

How much time was left to me before my jailer returned?

Taken by the savages, what could I do?

I could simply die now of pure fright and resignation as some animals do or I could gnaw my hand off at the wrist as other animals do.

As I sank my teeth into my own flesh, I cried silently and bitterly. As I tasted my own blood, I wanted to scream against this fate.

I would not accept fate!

Mountain men like Christopher Carson and Mike Fink never cried and they never accepted a fate they didn't like.

Have you any idea how tough and impervious the wrist is? Mine was nothing except tendon and veins and bone wrapped in a tough skin. I could not bite through even the first tendon before I got dizzy. I cringed from my own pain!

And I raged at myself for being weak!

And the lightning circled through my mind like electrified barbed wire!

The grey and silver clouds knocked their steaming heads together.

How much time was left before they buried me in a cell with a horde of other prisoners? Given time enough I could have slowly gnawed the wrist through, but no man can assault himself with such immediacy and with such a slow method of amputation. Given an axe, yes, I could have chopped it through immediately, but given the slow torture of tearing at my tendons with my teeth, a narcosis was needed, a nerve deadener to match the slow agony.

By now my body trembled in every muscle. Blood covered my face and leaked steadily from the wrist but my hand still would not pass through the steel circle.

Through the great black and silver tipped clouds boiling like grizzly bears fighting over a carcass, I thought clearly that all I could do was do my best. I could not go faster than the greater rhythm that timed my body, the greater clock and calendar that pulsed in my wrist, that fed the painkiller drop by drop into my nerves, and in effect determined my fate.

And then I heard the rough and straightforward voice of Red Knife. "Wait, Kit. Wait!"

"It is not easy to wait when I am trapped," I said.

He was at the window.

"Tell me where the trapper is," he said.

"He was drunk and filthy. How do I know where he went? Find him and kill him!"

"It is better that we should go with our plan all at the same time. But you must not feel the panic of the trap. It is going to take some time to do these things that must be done."

"What the blazes are you talking about?" I nearly screamed.

"One thing at a time. Sycamore knows and is helping us. By daylight tomorrow we will be in the mountains. First I must take the trapper with the key. Don't hurt yourself anymore."

His voice like granite settled my nerves and the grizzly bear clouds drifted away. I would wait. I would not make my pain any worse.

The thousands of stinging ants in my bloodstream slowly drifted off to their secret places.

"This room is on a hallway between the front and the back where the horses are," Red Knife said. "I will bring the trapper here."

"Please hurry, Red Knife," I said. "I cannot be a prisoner. I am not stoic like Jim Bridger or like Geronimo, a fool. I am a man who will soon die if he is not free."

"I go."

And I was alone again, but not without the reassurance of an ally. A man who has a dependable partner has a lot to count on in hard times. Now where was my wife?

"Kit, I am here at the window," she said.

I nearly cried.

"We are putting the things together that must be done to go west. We are going as fast as we can. I am even able to talk to Red Knife enough to complete a plan, but there are many policemen here."

"It looks impossible."

"No. As soon as Red Knife can isolate the man in drink, we will finish the battle. I think he will be with you soon. Now I must pack our camp for the long ride."

Alone again. It was crazy. I hadn't been able to figure out a safe way of riding off the island and westerly, how could she?

I tried to concentrate on a plan. I would settle for walking off the island no matter how hard it was. We could find other horses in other places. I would crawl off this crazy island if I could only be free of the savages that occupied it and make their crazy hives crazier every day.

Walk crawl swim or push a raft, just let me out!

My wrist ached now and the drying blood crackled on my face.

The light at the window faded. How long had I been a prisoner? A lifetime? A history?

I knew now that there was no way out of here except to take the key. Where was that man? Drunk and vomiting in the woods?

He had to return, because his partner knew I was here.

When?

Make a plan.

Red Knife had told me not to fight against my own strength. I had been crazy, beating my carcass to flinders and bleeding.

It was a lesson that should never be forgotten.

"He is coming," Red Knife whispered.

Red Knife stood in the shadows until I said, "You must kill him when he comes in."

"I have not brought the crossbow," he said.

The door opened. I hoped he would come in alone. And the Great Manitou did me that favor. He was still drunk but by now he was at bottom. His spirit was scarified and his eyes bulged with frustration and meanness.

Fine. The less he was using his head, the better for me.

He came to me and kicked me in the side as hard as he could.

"Why?" I asked.

"Because you're a goddamned rotten lazy lousy sonofabitch."

And he kicked me again. Ready this time, I fell away from his boot. Otherwise he'd have broken a rib.

"I have done nothing," I said.

"Hangin' around, watchin' a police station with a big goddamn knife ain't just nothin'," he smacked my face openhanded back and forth. I rolled with the blows as best I could, trying to appear to be an innocent weakling. I needed him close if Red Knife were to kill him.

"Now whada hell you doin' back in the brush? Huh!"

He came closer as Red Knife waited. The policeman couldn't see Red Knife's right hand slowly reach up from behind. Red Knife's arm was plaited with lean muscles like a cable. It was not the arm of a laborer, it was the arm of a wild person and it had the tensile strength of a boa constrictor.

The policeman turned and hit me smack on the nose with his fist, and I fell away from the punch.

"Coward," I said with as much hatred as I could put into my face.

"Yeah? You think so? Yeah!"

He was so excited he was careless and he came in close to drive his fist into my groin. I moved and he hit my hip.

Then Red Knife had his right arm around his throat, and the long plaited muscles squeezed down. He could not cry out, he could not scream or beg.

The arm slowly squeezed like a boa constrictor as the policeman's body started to contort and shudder and then to commence an Irish jig.

One arm, long and plaited. One neck bulging with blood.

How long? Maybe a minute or two he danced his Irish jig and then Red Knife let him fall at my feet.

He was not dead yet.

The keys! The keys!

Mixed in with dirty coins was my freedom.

Now we could move. I found a rope in the stable and quickly made a noose. Red Knife slipped the noose over the policeman's head, passed it over a beam and we hoisted the policeman onto a desk. Red Knife pulled the rope tight and tied it to the same stanchion I had been manacled to.

He came back and gently pushed the unconscious man off the desk so that he fell and dangled from the rope.

Red Knife counted coup.

We went out the door and I picked the two strongest horses. These were taken outside and their bridles tied to a tree. Quickly we opened the half doors and all the remaining horses moved

together into the corridor, maybe a dozen of them. It looked like a lot of horsemeat to me anyway.

Then we drove them out into the night. We slapped them and whipped them into stampeding into the park and darkness. They were beautiful heavy haunched and glossy sorrels and chestnuts.

The pounding of their hooves was smothered in the earth and lost in the noise of the constant traffic.

We ran on to our own horses, leaped upon them bareback and drove the horse herd farther into the woods and scattered them ahead of us.

The Great Manitou gave us the favor of being undiscovered.

When I thought the horses were scattered far and wide so that the policemen wouldn't know two were missing, we turned and raced toward camp. Now I prayed to the Great Manitou that Sycamore had a plan that would let us escape the island of savages.

She was waiting with our goods made up into two packs. The iron kettle was secure and the bear skin.

"Quickly," I said. "We must be off the island before daylight."

"Yes. Yes, Kit. I'm so pleased to see you free," and she cried and kissed me.

And I said, "There is no time for foolishness now, woman. We must run fast."

I laced the packs behind the saddles, knowing Red Knife would ride behind me.

When we were ready, she said, "Kit, here is my idea. We will act crazy like them. We will hide the brands on the hips of the horses and they will laugh at us because they will think we are crazier."

She brought out two halves of a white sheet that she had found somewhere and laid each one over the hips of the horses. On each sheet she had printed a sign in extra big letters:

NY TO LA

RIDING FOR JESUS

At first I couldn't understand it and when I did, I laughed and Red Knife laughed, and she quit crying and smiled.

Draped with the signs, we rode down the sidewalk and the people stared and shook their heads, and some offered us money and some laughed too, as we rode westerly and over the bridge to freedom.

RED KNIFE VALLEY

"WE WILL NEVER see the blood moon of the Absarokas if we fool around on the way," I said.

"Listen to me, Kit," Red Knife said over my shoulder, "if we haven't found the Spirit before we reach the mountains, we can't live anyway."

"What do you think?" I asked Sycamore, riding the mare.

"Red Knife has been with you so many years, surely you can trust his judgement."

"Allright," I said, begrudging the precious extra time, and turned the horse's head into the northwest wind that seemed to be mourning the same way every day across the Great Plains.

For awhile I thought the constant crying wind had unbalanced Red Knife. Usually he's the practical one, the killer.

But he'd grown moody. At night he scratched through the ploughed ground for flints or beads or bones.

79

When he found something, he'd withdraw into a silent, pro-
found meditation, and I couldn't disturb him, couldn't hurry him,
could hardly see him in the darkness that he brought over himself.

So we rode into the scrub and the dry washes of the Black Hills
where the Sioux believe their eternal Spirit sleeps and pray that it
will awaken before it's too late.

The first night we camped in an arroyo where there was water,
but precious little feed and the horses were already poor and weary
from the months we'd been going west.

Up from the arroyo a dry ridge trailed over into the next
twisting wash like a sleeping lizard. At the highest part of the
ridge, Red Knife found a circular depression surrounded by big
rocks. It looked like a small fort, and I reckoned it was some kind
of a lookout from the days before the whites came.

But Red Knife thought it had more meaning. I'd never seen
him look so troubled, his face reflecting an inner struggle, as if he
were trying to discover some great truth.

"Kit, when you sleep, I will come here. My lost Manitou is
here, but doesn't know me."

When I awakened at first light, he looked older. Maybe it was a
new line in his broad forehead, maybe it was the grey hair in his
long plait that had always been black as a crow. I looked into his
eyes and asked, "How was your night?"

"Something came to me, maybe a part of what I was once."

"How do you mean?"

"I know that praying place, I was there once, maybe a very
small boy with my people."

We saddled the hungry horses and with the sun rising behind
us, pressed on into the labyrinth of the sacred Black Hills.

All day Red Knife studied the wasteland, his eyes searching the high places, the caves created from displaced slabs of rock, and when we were lucky enough to find water, he sifted sand through his fingers as if he might turn up his own heart or an amulet containing the vision he wanted so much.

For me, I counted each day as so much distance we could travel before the meat and berries of the Absarokas were gone.

That night he found another sacred place and again our horses went on short rations.

After his night's vigil, Red Knife became even more solemn, more deep in his head, a state of thinking that was completely his own and something he could not share with me.

"I found another bead from my childhood that belongs to me," he said.

The lines in his forehead were maybe a shade deeper. Maybe there was more grey hair.

The next night the horses were poorer, our spare water was nearly gone, and the jackrabbit we ate was tough as whang leather, but Red Knife found another special spot high in the rocks.

In the morning he looked worn out.

"There is strong magic here," he said. "We must have it. Come there with me tonight."

"Spend all day lying around here?"

"It is necessary," he said. "We must not eat today. We must be pure for the night."

I was hungry enough already to eat raw cat, but I wanted to know the Great Spirit more than anything. So be it.

We found shade from a scrub pine and loafed while Sycamore looked for grass for the horses. All day, like lizards, we rested in

the shade. The only sounds came from stray crows and the haunting moan of the wind.

Shortly before sunset we climbed the barren rocky ridge and Red Knife showed me the praying place. Similar to the others in its simplicity, it might have had a brush arbor over it at one time. You'd never know it now because dust had collected on the floor, undisturbed for over a century. Red Knife ran his fingers through the dust and came up with a handful of grizzly bear claws, drilled to make a necklace.

"From a chief," Red Knife said, putting the claws in a leather pouch. "Maybe my father."

"How do you know?" I asked as we watched the sun balance on the western hills like a Mexican opal.

"I don't know. It may be I am my father," he murmured, expressing his bewilderment as to where he came from or where he was going.

The sun down, I felt the turning of the earth, the coming of the half moon, the sparkles in the unknown sky, and night came on us like a wave of warm water, a tidal broth from the deepest caverns of the undiscovered mind.

When we returned to the sun Red Knife sat with his legs crossed, staring at the pale dawn in the east. He looked tired, older, but his eyes were burning with some inner knowledge that had not been there before.

"We may leave now, Kit," he said quietly and rose like an emperor who knows every inch of his happy dominion.

It was odd. I realized that he was now more like a father to me than a brother. He was moving through time a lot faster than I. I could see it happening right in front of my eyes.

We rode west through the Bighorn country, avoiding the highways and barbed wire. Once in awhile we'd meet a cowboy riding a backroad and he'd tip his hat and say Howdy, and I'd nod likewise.

We camped in Montana that night. I felt the hurry-up quickening my blood and my body telling me it wanted to stop for a long rest.

Again Red Knife scouted the ground closely, examining fresh gopher mounds and when he'd picked up a couple arrowheads and some brass shell casings marked as Army ammunition, he lay down to rest as if the load he was carrying had grown heavier.

I worried more than ever. We used to share everything, but now he was becoming a separate person.

"You know, if I can help. . ." I said.

Closing his eyes he murmured, "I have slept here before. These flints are mine. My scars come from these shells. Maybe I died here."

"I'm glad you told me." I let it rest. He was on his own trail.

He could hardly wait to move out. He got up in the dark, had the fire going and the horses brought in before Sycamore and I awakened.

"We'll be there tomorrow." I tried to encourage her. She was slim as a willow wand before we started this trip, and now she was beginning to show sharp bones.

"I can go on as long as we must," she smiled.

"Maybe we find a rock wall in the way," Red Knife said. "Maybe we find a lake. We must not think of our journey as so many days. That is white man thinking."

"Time is the reason, Red Knife," I said. "The berries will be

gone soon, snow will fall, and the game moving away. We must find our place before we face a winter of hunger."

"You have the Great Spirit for the hunger you imagine," Red Knife said as we rode along, never stopping.

No matter how my bones ached or my butt sore, he meant to make some miles today.

Northwest. Always northwest. We came to a stream that seemed to go straight north and Red Knife decided to ride along with it. We came through hot sulfur springs that smelled worse than the city.

For the first time we saw a few elk, big brown animals, some with huge racks on their heads.

"We have no time to kill elk," Red Knife cautioned.

North into a long flat valley between two ranges of mountains. When we came to the meeting of our little stream with a much larger one, Red Knife spoke with conviction, "I know this river as I would know my own mother."

At the fork he turned upstream toward the high, formidable mountains that were already capped with snow.

"This is the Yellowstone River," I said, looking at my roadmap. "Over there's a cowtown named Livingston. Those mountains are the Absarokas."

"Yes," he smiled. "Yes, those are our mountains. This valley is Sioux country."

He bubbled with expectancy, with the joy of homecoming.

We were climbing into rougher country, more pleasing to me. The few houses became more real, the barns serving a purpose.

Red Knife seemed to be leading us straight into a steep wall of

mountains, a place where only mountain sheep could live. He was our guide, but he was a different man now. His hair was already iron gray, laced with strands of white. The lines in his face were deep grooves, like eroded cuts on the land. His eyes were still bright, but they looked off into the distance more and more, as if he perceived something coming that neither Sycamore or I could see.

And it was colder. A grey cloud massed in the north, a cloud that might bring snow by tomorrow.

"Yes," he nodded, "but we are close to home."

We entered a canyon and took a trail through big pines and climbed slowly across the side of the mountain.

We were into the Absarokas, those mountains of mystery that the Sioux regarded as a special place of magic and the whites after them always regarded with suspicion as if they'd scented an immortal and primeval animal lurking back in the passes and scarps.

They were uninhabited, touched only by a few trails that occasional trout fishermen used. The stream became smaller and soon there was not enough water to support even small trout. We could look back down and see the Yellowstone River wandering through Paradise Valley and the little houses with smoke and heat coming out of their chimneys.

The horses were bone weary, but no more than Sycamore or me either, for that matter.

Red Knife wouldn't stop. He watched the terrain closely, and once said, "The elk have started down."

"That's bad," I said. "We need to make our cache very soon."

"Yes. We need an elk and a bear. A few deer would be nice, too."

"And some smoked geese and ducks," I added, my mouth watering.

We'd been living on jackrabbits and windfall apples for a month.

"I'm not worried," Sycamore smiled. "I love these mountains. The chain saws haven't found the pines yet."

There would be little game this high because there was very little forage, and the air was thin and cold. The distant cloud in the north came on like a grazing grey roan mare.

We came through a pass in the great mountain which made two mountains and we found a well-used game trail, wide and even dusty from recent travel.

"Elk. Trail from summer to winter ground. Maybe a few old ones stay late."

The elk had followed the same easy trail for centuries, some of it worn deep into the ground and some wide enough for a wagon. Their hooves had churned up rocks like cobblestones.

There had been no sign of man either red or white for many miles.

A marmoset peered out from his den under a rock with bright little eyes. He would not make much of a meal. He whistled and backed into his den and we passed on by, saddles creaking, hooves knocking on the rocks.

Now we turned downward across the belly of the mountain, and we could see a small punchbowl valley with a small lake and also I thought I saw off to one side, a little cloud of mist.

Red Knife laughed. I don't remember if I ever heard him laugh like that before. It was a laugh of great satisfaction, a laugh of a man who has conquered impossible circumstances and come home with honor. He was so venerable now, so close to the Manitou, I did not feel like asking idle questions. The security that surrounded his saintly appeareance was enough for me.

I could imagine the Sioux dragging their travoix and herding their painted ponies down into the little valley, following the trail of the elk.

Late in the afternoon our trail broke out of heavy timber into the punchbowl. The ground was deep and black and a small stream wandered away into a landslide of boulders. It was a walled haven, unique, a magical place.

"There's a hot spring," Sycamore said.

I saw steam rising from a pool of clear water where salt had collected on the rocks. The salt had been licked and gnawed, but there was plenty left for us.

We could salt down our meat against the hardest times and we could bathe in the hot water!

Red Knife smiled at my excitement, and the worry lines on Sycamore's face eased off. She had put a lot of trust in my friend whom she couldn't even see.

We continued on across the little valley to the lake which swarmed with trout. Stopping to let the horses drink, I could imagine a dozen Sioux families camped here in tipis, their horses feeding, their children playing.

Red Knife said, "Let's go on to the cliff. My memory says to go there."

In the last of the sunlight we found the cave.

"Careful," he said. "Maybe a grizzly in there. We have been gone a long time."

"I hope he's big and fat," I said, loading up the car spring crossbow with a three foot length of rebar.

After lighting a pine knot torch, I gave the crossbow to Red Knife and entered the cave.

There was no bear, but it had been used as a den in the past and was rank with the smell. The walls were decorated with simple pictures and religious symbols, showing the history of the Sioux. There would be plenty of time to study them in the winter. Now it needed cleaning.

Outside, I looked at the grey sky and shivered.

"We'll starve before spring," I said.

"I didn't bring you here to starve," Red Knife said. "You may eat your brother the elk this winter."

"But the elk are gone."

"Maybe there is a way to bring one back."

I looked at his now ancient and wise face, and saw no hint of humor. He wasn't joking. But what did he mean? How could he bring an elk back to us?

"You have brought me back here," he said, and walked away.

Some time in the night a few flakes of snow fell upon us and in the morning our valley was white with a thin layer of snow that melted as soon as the sun came up.

Still, it was a warning of more to come, and the blood said to be ready.

Red Knife's hair had turned as white as the snow.

"This place is worth waiting for. How did you find it?" I asked.

"I don't know," he answered. "I know I was born here. I know I lived here until I was a blooded warrior. After I counted coup the first time, I don't remember so much."

"Did you spend winters here?"

"Yes. We had plenty of elk and buffalo and deer. In the winter we spent a lot of time in the cave, dreaming. The women were carrying their young and there were always dreams of babies coming.

"Yes."

I helped Sycamore bring hot mineral water to flood the cave. She cleaned the whole thing with a branch from a pine tree, and when she was satisfied that the cave was clean, I built a fire inside of juniper and sweet grass, not only drying it out but making the air clean and fresh.

Again we slept outside because she wanted our winter home to be properly ready.

In the morning, Red Knife put a few sticks on the fire and warmed his shriveled hands.

"I am old," he said slowly. "I will sleep the long sleep soon. Today I will bring the elk."

"Either that or we'll be only bones in the spring," I tried to make him smile, but he had no humor left in his spirit. I loaded up the crossbow with a length of rebar.

I put three more steel rods in the quiver, sharpened my big knife and was ready.

"We must take the hot bath and think of what this elk means to us besides meat," Red Knife said.

I followed him to the spring and soaked the badness out of me, my selfishness, my fear, the filth of the place we had left. Red Knife said I should think of the elk as a companion, a partner worthy of companionship. Not that our elk would come along like a dog and bow down and accept his death humbly. It was our duty to find enough humility to match his pride. If we had it, possibly we would meet. If not, the elk would continue on as he always did.

I lay back and saw the elk emerge in the stream. He was huge. Not ancient, not gristle and bone, he was like a great horse in his prime. His hide a rich brown almost orange, his antlers like frozen jagged lightning, his neck and shoulders brawny and unscarred. His eyes were fixed on something far away.

"I see him," I said.

"He is part of you."

"I understand that now."

"Then we are ready."

We came out into the cold air, dressed, and, taking the crossbow and quiver, we climbed the side of the mountain through the big pines where snow still remained.

We needed no artificial elk calls. If we were all in tune, we would meet.

We might kill him. He might kill us.

We climbed until we reached the broad trail and we rested there quietly, listening and smelling the sweet breeze.

I felt better. My saddle sores were healing. I needed to learn more to live here in the Absarokas, but if we had enough food nothing could happen to us that we couldn't handle. It was a feeling of being at home, secure and safe, ready to begin a new life.

We sat still and spoke mostly with hand signals in order to bring the elk to us. In this way I saw a grey fox creep by in pursuit of a small mouse. I saw the grouse come feeding by, their sentinels missing us completely. A young black bear rambled along through the bushes eating red berries.

The sun would leave soon but Red Knife never moved. His thick hair was the color of polished silver, the lines in his face those of an old man, and I noticed that his hands were losing flesh, leaving the skin to wrinkle and fingers to curl.

Paradise was not possible so long as my friend was wasting away before my eyes. I pondered a long time about how I might stop this development, but the more I thought, the more empty my answers.

I was ready to leave in the dusk, but Red Knife did not move. He stared at the trail that led on up the mountain. I had to learn that discipline because it was as important as breathing in this way of life.

It was not yet dark when I saw the elk far away through the pines. He browsed along, nibbling on the bearbrush and berry bushes. I could only see patches of orange at first, but as he came closer, I saw his rack of antlers, his eyes, his great shoulders.

The crossbow lay on my crossed legs, ready to fire.

Usually I let Red Knife kill because he is experienced, but if I passed the crossbow to him now, it would disturb this tranquility and the elk would simply lope away through the darkening pines.

Even lifting the crossbow to sight would be too much. I must wait and fire off my knees. I looked at Red Knife in my mind and saw his nod of approval.

The elk was so strong he had no reason to be in a hurry about anything. He was the king of his mountain, boss of the winds.

He came close enough for me to try a shot, but I was in the same hypnotic bubble that Red Knife was in, and I waited for something not of my own will to touch the trigger. We blended, the elk, Red Knife, and me. He was close enough for me to see his whiskers and his shoulder was in line with my knees.

Suddenly the crossbow snapped and the heavy rebar flew straight into his front ribs. There was no sound. He leaped high on his hind legs, rearing above me, his great blunt hooves ready to crush my bones, and in another instant those spears on his antlers would stab me into the ground.

Red Knife grabbed my arm and was rolling away under the low limbs of the pine trees.

The hooves came down, grazing my shoulder, and by the time the antlers came down we were on the other side of the tree. The elk stood and waited, feeling his death, the cold iron through his lungs, blood drowning him and spurting from his nostrils. He looked at us only a few feet away, crouched in the snow. His front legs collapsed and he settled down on his knees, his breath rasping. He lay his head down. Blood ran from his muzzle, his open eyes dusted with snow.

"Very good, Kit," Red Knife said. "You are ready to become a man of the Sioux."

With two fingers, he took blood from the muzzle of the elk and drew a band across my forehead. And he said a prayer in his language, affirming my coming into a manhood made up of skill,

patience, daring, strength, and magic. I stood as tall as I could and smelled the fresh blood and listened to the prayer as it entered my spirit.

"I thank you, Red Knife, for everything, for all of it."

Darkness had replaced the sun and the huge elk lay before us. We would be disrespectful to lose any part of it.

"I will stay here," he said, "and keep the scavengers away. You return in the morning with Sycamore."

It was the first time in many years that we had been separated. I wondered what it all meant. It was big. It was my life being made for me right under my nose and I didn't understand.

I saw the firelight near the cave, clambered down the rocky slide, and soon enough was home again.

Sycamore seemed to be so beautiful, waiting there by the fire. There was no fear in her, no worry that I wouldn't return, no dread of the outside.

She had the iron pot full of stew and wild turnips, spiced with wild herbs she'd found during the day.

"Red Knife?" she asked.

"With the elk."

"Then you are complete."

"More than that," I said, holding her to me, "we are complete."

We slept outside again. The cave would be there when it was needed, but we preferred the stars and the blood red moon coming over the eastern scarps.

The mood of achieving manhood had not passed from me. I felt like the elk reared back on his hind legs, his hind quarters

tensed, his great shoulders spread wide. I felt the urge the same as Sycamore, the slender thread of blood in the loins growing into a forest fire.

The immensity of the procreative spirit turned us into mewling kittens. I drifted away to sleep without dreaming. Sycamore was with child.

Before sunrise we were on the trail to Red Knife and the elk. We found the elk, but Red Knife no longer sat under the pine tree wrapped in his blanket. Now he lay alongside the elk, the blanket stretched over them both. Red Knife lay asleep with the elk and neither would awaken again.

The venerable old warrior had gone back to his ancestors, had returned to the Great Manitou where I could speak to him in the hard times, and he could watch over us in the valley of Red Knife for as long as we called it home.